Celebrate the S

Secret
Snowflak

Secret Snowflake

by
Taylor Garland

Little, Brown and Company
New York Boston

Little, Brown and Company

Hachette Book Group

1290 Avenue of the Americas, New York, NY 10104

Visit us at LBYR.com

First Edition: October 2017

Little, Brown and Company is a division of Hachette Book Group, Inc. The Little, Brown name and logo are trademarks of Hachette Book Group, Inc.

The publisher is not responsible for websites (or their content) that are not owned by the publisher.

ISBNs: 978-0-316-47246-3 (hardcover), 978-0-316-47248-7 (pbk), 978-0-316-47249-4 (ebook)

Printed in the United States of America

LSC-C

10 9 8 7 6 5 4 3 2 1

Chapter 1

"Snow day!"

Those two words were guaranteed to get Riley Archer out of bed, no matter how early it was. Riley's eyes flew open as she fumbled for her phone on the bedside table, then squinted at the screen. It was only 6:12—her alarm wasn't supposed to go off for another eighteen minutes—but Riley didn't mind the earlier-than-usual wake-up. Her little brother, Theo, was hollering about snow first thing in the morning; if there was going to be a snow day, Riley wanted to know about it!

Riley scrambled out of bed in such a rush that she forgot to grab her glasses. She'd been wearing glasses for a month, but she still wasn't quite used to them. Across the room, Riley yanked open the curtains and saw…nothing out of the ordinary. There was the deserted gray sidewalk, the stubby brown grass, and the empty black streets, which were etched with odd patterns where the salt trucks, in anticipation of a storm, had brined them overnight. It was early enough that the streetlights were still on, casting a weak yellow glow as the sky gradually began to lighten.

"What snow?" Riley mumbled to herself. But it wasn't like Theo to make up a story. She reached for her glasses and took another look.

Sure enough, in the warm glow of the streetlights, Riley could see it: little flurries drifting down from the leaden sky. She had to grin. Theo took everything so *literally*. Yes, it was snowing. But barely. Unless those faint flurries suddenly swirled into a blizzard, there was no way school would be canceled today. There wouldn't even be a late start.

And—to be completely and totally honest—that was okay with Riley. After all, it wasn't just any ordinary school day. It was the day Riley had been waiting for since September: the kickoff to Secret Snowflake! Ever since Riley had learned about Secret Snowflake on the first day of seventh grade, she'd been looking forward to it. Secret Snowflake was just one of the things that made Mrs. Darlington, Riley's homeroom and language arts teacher, so awesome. She was really into all kinds of different, creative assignments (Mrs. D. called them "alternative learning opportunities," whatever that meant). To Riley, the unusual projects were interesting, exciting, and sometimes even fun—and they made her really look forward to school.

Take Secret Snowflake, for example. In a few hours, the students in Mrs. Darlington's class would pick names and, over the next two weeks, exchange small, secret gifts. Sure, there was some schoolwork involved—they would have to write an in-class essay at the end of the project—but for the most part, Riley already knew that Secret Snowflake was going to be incredibly fun!

Might as well get ready for school, Riley thought. She'd already planned her outfit for today—an ice-blue sweater with her favorite skinny jeans and boots. As a finishing touch, Riley decided to wear her dangling snowflake earrings, too.

By the time Riley got downstairs, Theo was already eating a stack of waffles at the kitchen table. "Did you see?" he asked excitedly. "It's snowing! I bet school will be canceled!"

Riley paused to ruffle Theo's blond hair, grinning as he ducked away from her. "Flurries," she corrected him. "They're not going to cancel school for a light dusting of snow. But, who knows—we might have an early-release day if it picks up!"

Theo looked disappointed—but only for a moment. "It's still *snow*, Riley," he insisted. "That's better than nothing! And maybe it will get really heavy this afternoon and we can go sledding later."

"Sure," Riley said with a laugh. "Anything's possible."

After breakfast, Riley peeked into her backpack to make sure she had everything. Her binder, her books, her lunch money—check, check, and check. Most important, though, Riley had remembered to pack her personalized snowflake, the very first part of the Secret Snowflake assignment. At the start of the week, Mrs. Darlington had given each student a plain snowflake made out of heavy card stock and told them to decorate it to make it a reflection of their personalities. It was more challenging than it sounded, but Riley had really enjoyed the assignment. She had placed her school picture in the center of the snowflake and drew little branches around it. She used each branch to highlight a different interest—music notes because she loved to sing, a chocolate cupcake because she was a certified chocoholic, a photo of her family, and more. Then she'd filled in all the blank spaces with sparkly blue glitter because Riley loved sparkle. By the time she'd finished, Riley was really proud of her snowflake. Not only was it pretty enough that she planned to hang it in her room when she got to take it home, but it really did reflect her personality—and all the things that mattered most to her were represented on the snowflake.

"Bye, Mom! Bye, Dad! Bye, Theo!" Riley called as she wrapped her scarf around her neck. "See you after school!"

Then she paused in the doorway. Was it snowing harder already? "Or maybe before!" Riley added.

❄ ❄ ❄

By the time Riley got to homeroom, she could tell she wasn't the only one excited about Secret Snowflake. Some of the kids were trying to act cool, like they didn't really care, but almost everybody else was chatting excitedly about it. Riley's best friend, Sophia Perez, practically pounced on her the moment she walked through the door.

"Can you believe? Secret Snowflake? Is finally here?" Sophia asked breathlessly. Her excitement made it sound like she was asking a bunch of rapid-fire questions.

"I know!" Riley exclaimed. "And there are only two more weeks until Christmas break!"

"Come on! Let's hang up our snowflakes!" Sophia said as she pulled Riley across the room.

Together, the two girls hung their snowflakes on the window. The ledge under the window was crowded with labeled shoe boxes that would hold their Secret Snowflake presents.

"I wonder who will pick our names," Sophia said. "Tell the truth. Is there anybody you're hoping for?"

Riley shrugged. "Not really," she said, trying to sound casual. "I'd be happy with anybody."

Riley watched her friend to see if Sophia had noticed that Riley was keeping something from her. Because the truth was that Riley was hoping to pick someone in particular, and that someone was Marcus Anderson...the cutest and most interesting boy in school if you asked Riley. Of course, she'd be just as happy to have Marcus pick her. Either scenario sounded perfect. She'd had a crush on Marcus for almost two years now, and Secret Snowflake seemed like it would be the perfect chance to finally get to know him better and to show him how she really felt.

Luckily, Sophia's thoughts had already flitted off to another topic. "Do you think it will be hard? To come up with all the different presents?" she asked. "I mean, it would be easy if I pick your name. I know you so well! But what if I pick somebody who I don't know that well? What then?"

"That's what the snowflakes are for, I guess—to give a few hints," Riley replied. "Plus, I think that's supposed to be part of the challenge. Getting to know your person a little better and all that."

Just then, Marcus entered the room, with Mrs. Darlington right behind him. "Good morning, class," Mrs. Darlington announced. "If you haven't already hung your snowflake on the window, please do so now. Then go ahead and take your seats."

Riley hurried across the room to her desk, tucking her hair behind her ears as she snuck a glance at Marcus. He was standing by the window, goofing with Austin as the boys hung up their snowflakes. She didn't want Marcus to catch her staring...but if he happened to glance her way at the same time, well, that would be pretty incredible.

She watched closely to see which snowflake was Marcus's, just in case she picked his name. And even if she didn't, she still planned to check it out later so she could find out more about him.

As the bell rang, Mrs. Darlington placed a small silver box on her desk. "And now, the moment we've all been waiting for," she announced with a big smile. "I've placed each of your names on slips of paper inside this box. One by one, I'll call you to come pick a name for your Secret Snowflake. Remember, once you pull a name, you're sworn to secrecy! No telling anyone whose name you picked. We'll go in alphabetical order. Marcus Anderson."

Riley watched as Marcus got up from the seat in front of her, ambled across the classroom, and pulled a slip of paper out of the box. He read it, smiled, and slipped it into his pocket. Then he looked right at Riley—and smiled again!

Why did he do that? Had Marcus picked her name? Was he giving her a *sign*?

Riley's heart was pounding with such anticipation that she almost didn't hear Mrs. Darlington call her name.

"Riley Archer," Mrs. Darlington repeated. "Riley?"

The class started to giggle.

Riley didn't care, though. Marcus Anderson had *smiled* at her! She hurried up to the front of the room, thrust her hand into the box, and shut her eyes. Her fingers closed around a scrap of paper and, with her heart still pounding, Riley pulled it out.

Who would be her Secret Snowflake?

Riley was about to find out!

Chapter 2

In her rush to unfold the slip of paper, Riley's fingers fumbled, and the tiny scrap of paper fluttered away from her as if carried by a breeze. Riley made a wild lunge and grabbed the paper just before it hit the floor. She was so eager to open it that she didn't even notice that a few kids in class were laughing again.

Relax, Riley told herself sternly, forcing her heart to stop pounding, her fingers to stop trembling. Then, holding her breath, she unfolded the paper and read:

MARCUS ANDERSON

Riley blinked in disbelief. She wasn't imagining it, right? A second glance at the paper confirmed what she'd seen the first time. Riley could feel the smile spread across her face. Her Secret Snowflake was *Marcus Anderson*! It was perfect—no, it was *too* perfect—no, it was *beyond* perfect—

"Riley," Mrs. Darlington said, and from the sound of her voice, Riley had a feeling that it wasn't the first time Mrs. Darlington had called her name.

"Yes?" Riley said quickly, looking up at Mrs. Darlington through her glasses.

Mrs. Darlington looked like she was trying not to smile. "You may sit down," she said. Then she turned back to the class and called, "Becca Brandt!"

Too late, Riley realized that she'd been holding up the Secret Snowflake selection process. She scurried to her seat, sneaking a look at Marcus as she passed by his desk. She wanted to flash him the same kind of smile he'd sent her way. But he was scribbling something on the cover of his notebook, not paying any attention.

Riley slid into her seat, still beaming. She glanced over at all the personal snowflakes on the wall, trying to get a better look at Marcus's snowflake. From where she was sitting, it didn't look like it had much detail. It just looked like it had been hastily colored in blue with some red stripes. But Riley was sure that, upon closer inspection, she'd see some cool details that Marcus had put on the snowflake to represent his personality.

Mrs. Darlington was talking about their Secret Snowflake essays, which meant that Riley *really* needed to pay attention so that she didn't miss anything important.

But it wasn't always easy to pay attention, not with Marcus sitting right in front of her. She stared at the back of his neck, where he had five freckles visible below his reddish-brown hair.

Quit it, Riley told herself, and focused all her attention on Mrs. Darlington.

"This project has many parts—not unlike the spokes of a snowflake," the teacher was saying. "But most important, I think, is what you will learn about the nature of giving. There's a famous expression, dating back thousands of years: 'To give is better than to receive.' For your homework tonight, I'd like you to write about that saying. Do you agree? Disagree? Why?"

Riley studiously made some notes.

"Please don't tell anybody the identity of your Secret Snowflake," Mrs. Darlington continued. "Even if you think you're just telling one person, you'd be surprised how quickly news can spread. I promise it's a lot more fun to wait until the big reveal at the Christmas party on the last day of school before break."

TOP SECRET, Riley scribbled in her notebook, underlining the words three times for emphasis.

"Finally, as we work on the Secret Snowflake project, try to find out how you can be the best possible friend," Mrs. Darlington continued. "There's no one way to be a great friend. I hope, by the end of this assignment, you'll all be more aware of what it feels like to be the best friend you can be."

Best friend I can be, Riley wrote. That wouldn't be hard. After all, Riley already knew that Marcus deserved the best Secret Snowflake—and she was up for the challenge!

❄ ❄ ❄

At lunch, Riley scoured the cafeteria for Sophia. Since Sophia always brought lunch from home, she saved a pair of seats while Riley waited in line for hot lunch. But Sophia wasn't at any of their usual tables with the other seventh-grade girls. Instead, she was sitting at the end of a nearly empty table, where a few sixth graders looked at her curiously.

Riley and Sophia made eye contact, and Sophia waved her over.

"Hey," Riley said as she put her tray on the table. It was Pizza Friday, and there was a slab of cake, too. Not bad at all, as far as cafeteria food went. "Why are we sitting over here?"

"So we can talk Secret Snowflake, of course," Sophia replied in a dramatic whisper.

Riley frowned a little. "We can't talk Secret Snowflake," she said, also speaking in a hushed voice. "Mrs. Darlington said we were sworn to secrecy."

Sophia waved her hand in the air. "Other people, maybe, but not you and me," she said confidently.

"We're best friends! We don't have any secrets from each other! Besides, I really need your help."

Riley was torn. On the one hand, Mrs. Darlington couldn't have been more clear with her instructions. But on the other hand, the teacher had also told the students to be the best friends they could be.

Sophia, noticing Riley's hesitation, kept talking. "It only matters if we pulled each other's names," she said. "I didn't pull your name. So did you pull my name?"

"No," Riley admitted.

"Great!" Sophia said brightly. "Then there's no problem. So—spill it. Whose name did you pick?"

Riley glanced around to make sure no one would overhear her. Luckily, they were sitting near the back of the noisy, bustling cafeteria, and the sixth graders at the other end of the table weren't paying any attention to them. Riley leaned closer to Sophia and whispered, "Marcus Anderson."

"Really?" Sophia squealed so loudly that Riley reached out and grabbed her wrist.

"*Shhhh!*" Riley hissed. "People are looking!"

"Sorry," Sophia said in a quieter voice. "You're just so lucky, Riley. I wish I'd picked my crush."

Riley sat up extra straight, a look of alarm on her face. "Wait—wait—" she stammered. "How did you know?"

"How did I know?" Sophia repeated. "How could I *not* know? We're best friends, remember? You didn't have to say anything for me to figure it out."

Riley swallowed hard. "Do I—do I make it really obvious?" she asked.

She almost didn't want to know the answer.

"Oh, no, definitely not," Sophia assured her. "Seriously. I mean it."

"Because you'd tell me if I did, right?" Riley said.

"Of *course* I would," Sophia said firmly. "I can only tell because I know you so well. You get this look on your face whenever you see him ... all smiley-happy, like everything is awesome, even if Mr. Jessup is talking about the history test."

Riley laughed a little. It was no secret to anybody in seventh grade that she thought history class was a total bore.

"If you were *too* obvious, don't worry, I'd tell you," Sophia promised. "That's what BFFs are for."

And as the girls exchanged a smile, Riley knew that Sophia was telling the truth.

"Have you figured out what you're going to give Marcus?" Sophia continued. "That must be a lot of pressure, huh? You want the gifts to be *perfect*, but not *too, too* perfect, and definitely not too expensive...."

"Actually, I already decided that I'd make all of the Secret Snowflake gifts," Riley confided.

Riley thought it was a brilliant idea. Her whole family was really into making gifts, and she knew from experience that a handmade, one-of-a-kind present was a very special thing indeed.

But from the look on Sophia's face, Riley suddenly wondered if other people felt the same way.

"Are you sure?" Sophia asked dubiously. "I mean— are you planning to make *all* of them?"

"Well, yeah—that's what I was thinking," Riley said. She poked at her cake with her spork, suddenly feeling a lot less hungry. "What's wrong? Is that a bad idea?"

"No," Sophia said. Even Riley could tell that she was choosing her words very carefully. "It's just— I think everybody else will be doing store-bought stuff. Like key chains or comic books or gifts cards. You know. That kind of thing."

Riley's shoulders relaxed. "That's just it!" she exclaimed, before remembering to lower her voice. "*Everybody* will be doing that—but Marcus isn't everybody. He's special, and I want all his Secret Snowflake presents to be special, too. You know what I mean?"

"I guess," Sophia said.

"Besides, I can *make* a key chain for Marcus," Riley said airily. "And it will be cool and unique and awesome, just like him."

"You're lucky you're so crafty," Sophia said. "If I made anything for my Secret Snowflake, it would probably look like a kindergartner did it."

"Don't say that!" Riley said, trying not to laugh. "Besides, if you want to make something, I can help you. It will be fun!"

"First I have to figure out *what* to make—or buy," Sophia said glumly. "Which is practically impossible."

"Why?" asked Riley.

Sophia leaned forward. "Because my Secret Snow-flake is Alice Scofield!" she groaned. "I don't know where to begin."

Riley made a sympathetic face. She understood why Sophia was struggling, but it wasn't the end of the world. Alice was a new student at Hampton Creek Middle School—not Sophia's worst enemy or something like that.

"I don't know *anything* about her, and she doesn't talk to anyone, ever," Sophia continued. "After gym, in the locker room, I heard Marian say that she thinks Alice is really stuck-up and hates Hampton Creek and wants to go back to Hawaii."

"How would Marian even know that?" Riley replied. "You just said that Alice doesn't talk to anybody."

"Maybe she doesn't talk to anybody because she's stuck-up and she hates it here," Sophia said.

"Or maybe because she's shy and homesick?" Riley suggested.

"Maybe," Sophia said, nodding. "But how do you give special gifts to a complete and total stranger?"

"That," Riley said, "is the Secret Snowflake challenge!"

"Still, even though I know practically nothing about Alice, it's easier than if I picked some random guy," Sophia continued. "Probably even easier than if I had picked my crush, now that I think about it."

"Why's that?" asked Riley.

"Well, I mean, boys are weird," Sophia said. "Who knows what they like? Do *you* know what they like?"

"Uh…" Riley began.

"Exactly," Sophia said. "At least with girls, you can always get hair stuff or nail polish or whatever. It's generic, but it's fine."

"I don't know about that," Riley said. "It's Secret Snowflake. It's not supposed to be generic—it's supposed to be special. That's the whole point—to be the best friends we can be, no matter who we're paired with."

The bell rang then, and everybody started to pack up their trash.

"Why do I suddenly get the feeling that Secret Snowflake is going to be a lot more work than we thought?" asked Sophia.

Chapter 3

After school, Riley wanted to get right to work on making a list of Secret Snowflake gifts for Marcus, but first she had a 3C rehearsal. The Christmas Carol Chorus—or 3C—was one of Riley's favorite after-school activities, but it only lasted for about month, from right after Thanksgiving to the start of Christmas break. Riley wouldn't miss a 3C rehearsal or performance for anything.

Mr. Macintosh—most of the kids called him Mr. Mac—was the music teacher at Hampton Creek Middle School, and he was the kind of person who was ridiculously happy 365 days a year. Add in the holiday season, and Mr. Mac's cheerfulness cranked up to level 11. He was whistling a carol when Riley arrived at rehearsal.

"Riley Archer!" Mr. Mac's booming voice rang through the music room.

"Hi, Mr. Mac," Riley said as she grabbed her music folder.

"Big day, huh?" he said, his eyes twinkling. "I heard Secret Snowflake is in full swing."

"What's in full swing?" someone asked from the doorway.

Riley turned around to see Jacob Richards standing there. Even though she and Jacob had been lab partners since September, she didn't know him very well. She was surprised when he'd showed up for the first 3C rehearsal, since he hadn't been in the chorus last year.

"Hey, Jacob," Riley called with a little wave. "We were just talking about Secret Snowflake."

"Of course," Jacob replied. "The number one topic of conversation in seventh grade today. Happy with who you picked?"

Riley nodded, making sure not to smile too much. She was still painfully aware that Sophia had guessed her crush—and she didn't want to make the same mistake twice. "How about you?" she asked.

"Very happy," Jacob said—and then he changed the topic of conversation. "Mr. Mac, when's our next performance?"

"It's on Wednesday," Mr. Mac replied. "We'll be singing at the Hampton Creek Mall, near Santa's Workshop."

"Sounds fun," Jacob said. A few eighth graders filed into the room. They didn't even look over when Riley called out hi. Then again, they never talked to *anybody* else. That was why the other kids had started calling them Squad Eight, since they traveled in a totally exclusive pack.

"You know, I don't want to brag, but I guess you're lucky I'm here," Jacob said with a playful smile.

"Oh, really?" Riley teased. "Why is that?"

"Because otherwise, you would be the *only* seventh grader in 3C," Jacob told her.

Riley placed her hand over her heart. "A fate worse than death!" she joked.

"Pretty much. I mean, everybody knows that

Squad Eight over there would eat a lone seventh grader alive," Jacob said.

Riley glanced over to where the eighth graders were clustered around someone's cell, completely oblivious to everyone else in the room. "Oh yeah," she said with a laugh. "Everybody knows that. They're vicious."

"So then you'd have to form, like, an alliance with the sixth graders," Jacob said. "If they'd even let you in their tribe."

"Whoa. I didn't know they had a *tribe*," Riley said. "This is even more serious than I thought."

Mr. Mac played a few chords to get everyone's attention. "Okay, 3C," he announced. "Let's get this rehearsal started."

Riley was still smiling as she hurried over to her place on the risers. She'd never noticed before how funny Jacob could be.

By the time Riley caught the late bus home, the snow was getting heavier—and Theo was thrilled!

They had just enough time for a quick snowball fight before dinner. Then Mom was rapping on the kitchen window to tell them to come in. The house seemed even cozier than usual as Riley stomped her feet in the entryway, knocking clumps of snow off her boots.

"Mmm, something smells good," Riley called out. "What's for dinner?"

"Spaghetti and meatballs," Mom replied. "Plus, I made brownies for dessert."

"Brownies! Brownies! Brownies!" Theo cheered. He was almost as big a chocolate fanatic as Riley... almost!

After dinner, Riley was clearing the table when Dad glanced out the window. "It's really coming down out there," he said. "Good thing tomorrow's Saturday. If you two had school, there would definitely be a snow day."

"Too bad," Riley groaned. "Snow days on the weekend are a total waste."

"It's still a snow day, even if it's Saturday," Theo said. He had chocolate smears on his face from the brownie. "We can build a fort and make a snowman and have another snowball fight! And go sledding!"

Riley had to smile at her overexcited little brother. "We can definitely do *some* of those things," she told him. "But I'm also going to be busy making presents for my Secret Snowflake."

"That's right!" Mom exclaimed. "I almost forgot that Secret Snowflake started today. Who did you pick?"

Riley shrugged. "Just some guy, Marcus," she said casually. "Mrs. Darlington told us that the goal of the assignment is to figure out how to be the best friend we can be. So I think I'm going to make all of Marcus's presents."

"Wow," Mom said. "That's a lot of work—and a very special gesture."

"I know!" Theo spoke up. "You could make him an ornament when we have our ornament-making party!"

"Great idea, Theo!" Riley said. "Thanks!"

It was an Archer family tradition to make new ornaments for their Christmas tree every year—

and one of Riley's favorite holiday memories. She'd already sketched a picture of the ornament she wanted to make this year: a felt snowman holding a cup of cocoa.

"I was thinking we could watch a movie after dinner," Mom said. "How does that sound? Family movie night!"

"Can I pick?" Theo asked right away.

"Sure," Riley said with a shrug. "I might not have time for a movie, though. I really want to get started on my Secret Snowflake presents."

"But it's family movie night," Theo said.

"Well, I can watch the beginning while I work, I guess," Riley told him. "But you can still pick, since I probably won't watch the whole thing."

After the dishes were done, Riley completed her homework assignment for Secret Snowflake and changed into her favorite pajamas—the ones with polar bears on the pants and a velvety snowflake on the shirt—and curled up on the couch with her notebook and feather-topped pen. She stared thoughtfully into the distance.

I guess I could make a list of what I know about Marcus, she realized. *And then I could use that list to figure out what gifts he might like.*

Riley started to write.

Stuff Marcus Likes

sports (all sports? def. soccer!!!)
gum
robotics club
red (I think? red backpack)
superhero stuff
comic books

Riley stared at her list and frowned a little. Was that really all she knew about Marcus—even though she'd been sitting behind him for months? She had to wonder if he was working on a Secret Snowflake present right now, too...and if he'd really picked her name like she suspected. Thinking about that was only a distraction, though, and Riley didn't have time for distractions.

I guess I actually don't know all that much about

Marcus, she thought. Now she understood a little better why Sophia was so disappointed about choosing Alice. It was tricky to plan a bunch of presents for someone you barely knew.

Riley tried to shrug off her concerns. *Remember, this is the whole point of Secret Snowflake*, she told herself. *To get to know the person better so you can be the best possible friend to them.* She'd managed to get a better look at Marcus's snowflake after lunch, but the way he chose to decorate it didn't reveal much about his personality. Even upon close inspection, Riley saw that he'd simply colored it blue with some red stripes. She was pretty sure the design was based on his favorite baseball team's jersey, but she couldn't be sure. Maybe he just liked the pattern? A small part of Riley wondered if it meant something that Marcus hadn't put a lot of effort into decorating his snowflake, but she banished that thought from her mind almost immediately. *Maybe Marcus isn't artistic*, she told herself. *Or maybe he was really busy and didn't have a lot of time to spend on the assignment.* She'd just have to use her detective skills to find out more about Marcus!

First, though, Riley needed to figure out something to make for Marcus based on what she already knew about him. She definitely wanted to have a present ready to deliver on Monday morning. Theo's ornament idea was good, but the family ornament-making party wasn't for a few more days.

Maybe a key chain! Riley suddenly thought as she remembered one of Sophia's suggestions. She glanced down at the list and read *soccer.* Marcus was on the soccer team at school. Riley had never been to any of the games, but she'd heard him talk about it plenty of times before homeroom started. From the way the other boys talked, it sounded like Marcus was the star of the team

I could use modeling clay to make a soccer ball, Riley thought excitedly. *Maybe with a little crown on top—since Marcus is king of the Soccer Field! And I can attach a key ring and a chain, and then I'll have made a custom key chain, just for Marcus—the only one like it in the whole world.*

Riley put her pen down with a satisfied smile.

It was time to get to work!

In her bedroom, Riley scrounged around for everything she would need. Last year, she'd been totally obsessed with making clay charms and had spent her allowance buying different colors of modeling clay and lots of intricate tools. While Riley had been too busy with school stuff to make a charm since last summer, she was glad for all the practice she'd had, especially with using the clay sculpting tools. She was confident that she could make a really cool-looking key chain for Marcus.

Back at the kitchen table, Riley rolled a chunk of white clay between her palms until it formed a perfectly round ball. Then she held the black clay in her fist to soften it a little. Working with black clay was tricky; the dye was so intense that it would stain her hands and could easily transfer to the white parts of the soccer ball, making it a smudgy, smeary mess. Riley had learned that lesson the hard way when she'd tried to make a clay Dalmatian puppy. This time, though, she knew better and would be extra careful.

When the black clay was soft and pliable from the

warmth of her hands, Riley rolled it into a thin sheet. Then, using her cutting tool, she carefully sliced it into evenly sized pentagons.

Next came the tricky part—transferring the pentagons to the white ball without transferring smudges of color, too. Luckily, Riley had the perfect tool in her collection. She was concentrating so hard that she didn't even notice that she was biting her lower lip.

At last, the final pentagon had been transferred. With just enough pressure, Riley pushed on each one to attach it to the ball. She beamed at the tiny soccer ball in her palm. It looked like the real thing—just in miniature!

Riley put the soccer ball to the side and made a crown out of yellow clay, which she attached to the top of the soccer ball. "Mom? Can I use the oven?" she called after she'd achieved the perfect shape for the crown.

"What for?" asked Mom.

"I made a clay thing and it's ready to be fired," Riley explained.

"Oh, sure," Mom replied. She joined Riley in the

kitchen and helped her preheat the oven while Riley carefully placed the delicate clay soccer ball on a tray. After it spent some time in the hot oven, the soccer ball would be as hard as a rock—and durable enough to attach to a key chain. It wouldn't get any chips or dings, even if it bounced around in Marcus's backpack under a pile of heavy textbooks.

Right before Riley baked the charm, she remembered to make a hole in it with a wooden skewer so that she could attach it to a key chain after it was finished. Then she slid the tray into the oven.

"How long should I set the timer for?" asked Mom.

"An hour should be long enough," Riley said, peeking through the oven window to make sure the soccer ball hadn't rolled off the tray. After the clay charm had hardened and cooled, Riley would coat it with clear glaze and screw the key chain attachment into the small hole. It was a lot of steps, but Riley wasn't worried about how long it would take.

Waiting until Monday to sneak it into Marcus's Secret Snowflake mailbox?

Now *that* would be a difficult wait!

Chapter 4

Riley set her alarm for even earlier than usual on Monday morning so that she could get to school before anyone else. She couldn't *wait* to deliver Marcus's new key chain! But she wanted to be extra careful so that no one would see her do it—and spoil the surprise.

Luckily, Mrs. Darlington was the only one in the classroom when Riley arrived. She smiled knowingly as she said, "Good morning, Riley! I can imagine what brought you here so early."

Riley grinned, then put her finger to her lips and whispered, "Shhhh!"

Mrs. Darlington laughed. "Don't worry, your secret is safe with me," she promised.

Riley hurried across the room and pulled a small package out of her pocket. After the key chain was finished, Riley had carefully wrapped it in dark blue tissue paper, sealed with a single snowflake sticker.

With a fast glance over her shoulder to make sure no one was watching, Riley slipped the key chain into Marcus's Secret Snowflake box and quickly closed the lid. That was it—over and done in a matter of seconds. And no one, except Mrs. Darlington, was any the wiser!

"Mission accomplished," Mrs. Darlington joked. "Bravo!"

"Thanks," Riley said, pressing her hand across her chest. "Why is my heart still pounding?"

"Adrenaline, probably," Mrs. Darlington said. "You were all pumped up! It will take a minute to fade. Don't worry, I've seen this before. It gets easier."

Riley wanted to believe Mrs. Darlington, but

that honestly sounded impossible. She was about to respond when a couple other kids came into the room, glancing around furtively. She spotted Jacob and gave him a little wave. Riley tried to hide her smile. She had a feeling that he'd had the same idea—get to school early and deliver a present on the sly!

Before she went back to her desk, Riley decided to peek in her own Secret Snowflake mailbox. She didn't have high hopes—it was obvious that she'd been the first student to arrive—but she figured it wouldn't hurt to check.

Sure enough, though, the mailbox was empty. Riley tried to ignore the surprising pang of disappointment she felt. *It's too early*, she told herself. *No one else is even here yet. Besides, you might not even get a present today.*

Then Riley heard someone call her name. Sophia was standing in the doorway, waving wildly.

"Hey! Morning!" Riley said as walked over to her desk.

"Riley!" Sophia said again. She dropped her backpack on the floor with a loud *thud* and perched on the edge of Riley's desk. "Did you do it? Did you deliver it?"

Riley glanced around to see if anyone was watching, then nodded. "Mrs. Darlington saw me, but that's it," she replied.

"Nice!" Sophia said as she held up her hand for a high five.

Riley high-fived her, then dropped her hand fast. "Come on—we have to be more careful," she said. "He's not here yet, but..."

"Oh! Of course! I hear you," Sophia said. "Sorry."

"I just don't want anyone to figure it out and tell him," Riley explained. "Of course, if *he* figured it out on his own..."

Riley's voice trailed off as she imagined what that would be like. Incredible...and also terrifying... What would Marcus say? How would he guess? Would it be because she accidentally gave it away...or because he was paying extra-close attention to her? Then she remembered the way Marcus had smiled at her after he pulled a name from the silver Secret Snowflake box...a special smile that seemed like it was meant just for her....

"Earth to Riley. Come in, Riley," Sophia joked.

"Huh? What?" Riley asked, jolting back to reality.

"You drifted off to outer space for a minute," Sophia said.

"Sorry. I just got distracted," Riley said. Then she decided to change the subject. After all, Marcus sat right in front of her, and he could arrive at any moment. And one thing Riley knew for certain was that she did *not* want to be responsible for revealing the secret before the big party.

"So...do you have anything to deliver today?" Riley asked pointedly.

Sophia sighed so loudly her bangs fluttered. "No," she admitted. "I even went to the Hampton Creek Mall yesterday to shop and everything. But how do you buy something for somebody you don't even know?"

Riley glanced around uneasily. "We should not be talking about this," she said. "Someone could overhear us and figure it out."

Then Riley had an idea. She grinned at Sophia as she pulled out her phone and sent her a text.

Riley: Let's text about it. This way nobody will know what we're talking about

Sophia: genius!!!

Riley: So...about Alice...

Riley: You could always get her some cute pencils or something like that

Sophia: Maybe. But if everybody else is getting these incredible, unique, personal gifts and Alice gets a pack of pencils?

Riley: good point. What about Alice's snowflake? Did you check it out?

Sophia: yeah. It's basically all beach photos. I think they're from her old hood, back in Hawaii.

Sophia: I can't exactly give her the beach, can I?

Riley glanced over at the window. Even from a distance, she could see that Alice's snowflake was covered in tropical scenes.

Riley: yeah … probably can't give her the beach …

Riley: but u know what? Alice is probably not used to snow

Riley: this whole "winter" thing is a totally new phenomenon for her. maybe you could give her something to help her get used to it!!!!

It seemed like a fine suggestion to Riley, so she was surprised when Sophia started cracking up—until Riley read Sophia's next message.

> **Sophia:** Like what? Gloves?

> **Sophia:** Or maybe socks? What an awesome Secret Snowflake gift! Who wouldn't want a pair of nice new socks???

By then, Riley was laughing, too. She was starting to understand why Sophia was having such a hard time picking out presents for Alice.

Riley glanced over to the window—and realized that Marcus was standing there, messing around with Ben and Austin. With the flurry of texts, she hadn't even noticed when he'd arrived at school. If Marcus had checked his Secret Snowflake mailbox and found his present, Riley had missed it...and if he'd left something in *her* mailbox, she'd missed that, too.

The bell rang, but everyone was chatting so much that no one seemed to notice. Mrs. Darlington raised an eyebrow at the class as she clapped her hands loudly.

"Good morning, everybody!" she announced. "I know we're in a state of serious Secret Snowflake excitement, but we've got a lot of material to cover today. So if you'd all sit down and get ready for class to begin..."

There was a rush of activity as the students scurried to their desks. Riley reached into her backpack and pulled out her notebook. She'd lost track of time while she and Sophia texted; Riley had hoped to check her Secret Snowflake mailbox again before the start of class. Now it was too late. It probably didn't matter, anyway. Riley guessed that Marcus—or whoever had picked her name for Secret Snowflake—wouldn't be quite so bold to deliver a present while she was right there in the room and could notice at any moment. Besides, Riley could come back to Mrs. Darlington's room and check her mailbox after school. Then again, Riley knew she should try to be patient. There was no rule that Secret Snowflake gifts *had* to be exchanged on the very first day.

Riley couldn't help herself. She snuck a peek at her mailbox....

And realized that the lid was slightly ajar!

Riley's heart started beating faster. She knew she'd closed the lid firmly after she'd checked—she *knew* it. Which meant that someone *else* must've opened it. To put something inside?

Of course to put something inside! she thought excitedly. *No one would just go around looking in someone else's mailbox for fun—right?*

Now Riley was dying to run across the room and grab her mailbox. But she could never do that. Everyone would laugh, for one thing—and Mrs. Darlington would *not* be happy. No, Riley didn't have a choice. She'd just have to sit there, waiting patiently until the bell rang. Then, if she was really quick, she could probably check it before she went to math class.

It was the longest fifty minutes of Riley's life. She tried so hard to pay attention to the lesson, but one part of her brain was totally distracted, wondering *what* was in her mailbox...and *who* had left a surprise for her.

At long last, the bell rang. Riley immediately shoved all her stuff in her backpack. As the rest of her classmates swarmed to the door, Riley moved in the opposite direction—toward the windows and the Secret Snowflake mailboxes. She didn't even realize she was holding her breath as she eased open the lid—it was on, just crooked—and peeked inside.

There was a gold-wrapped present inside.

Riley pulled the thin parcel out of her mailbox. It hardly weighed a thing, but the wrapping was so pretty she wished she didn't have to remove it.

But Riley's eagerness to find out what was inside the present quickly won out. She used the edge of her fingernail to carefully pry up the tape; the gold paper was so pretty she'd keep it and add it to her scrap-paper collection at home. Maybe she could use it in a collage or to make a Christmas card.

Then Riley unwrapped the present and discovered ten sheets of glitter paper! There were two in each color: red, green, silver, gold, and blue. Even under the greenish-yellow fluorescent lights of the classroom, they sparkled with a brilliant intensity. Riley couldn't *wait* to make something with them!

Something fluttered to the floor. It wasn't one of the heavy, glitter-coated card-stock pieces; no, it was something lighter and more delicate. Riley leaned down and picked up a small scrap of paper with scalloped edges.

she brings sparkles wherever she goes—

sparkles on her nails and sparkles on her toes

this paper seemed like the perfect surprise

for the sparkly girl and her sparkly eyes

Riley blinked, then read it again.

No one had ever written a poem for Riley before. But that wasn't the only reason she felt all trembly and giddy inside. Her Secret Snowflake gift was, well, *perfect* for her. Whoever had picked it must have noticed that Riley wore glitter-frame glasses and that most of her accessories—even her sneakers—had sparkles. They'd even noticed how much she liked making stuff. Why else would they have picked out craft supplies for her? That's when Riley realized that whoever had written the poem—whoever had pulled her name for Secret Snowflake—*knew* her.

And that, Riley realized, was a very special thing.

Chapter 5

At 3C rehearsal that afternoon, Riley sang her heart out. It was easy to do, when she was filled with so much happiness from her Secret Snowflake surprise.

Before the end of practice, Mr. Mac had some big announcements. "Remember, we're performing at the Hampton Creek Mall Wednesday afternoon," he said. "Try to be there no later than four-thirty—we'll start singing at five o'clock sharp."

One of the sixth graders raised her hand. "Where are we meeting?" she asked. "The mall is, like, pretty big."

"Not at the food court, I hope," Jacob whispered

near Riley's ear. She elbowed him to keep quiet—Mr. Mac was pretty laid-back, but even he didn't appreciate it when students messed around during rehearsal or announcements.

"We'll meet at the food court," Mr. Mac said.

Riley choked back her laugh. This time, Jacob elbowed her.

"What's wrong with the food court?" Riley asked him. "I mean, I know it doesn't compare to, like, the Cupcakery, but it's still got some good stuff."

"I was just messing around," Jacob replied. "I love the food court. I'm basically going to eat all the fries. I can't resist fries. Ever."

"Our actual performance will be in the plaza, right in the middle of the mall. That's where the pictures with Santa is set up, as well as the gift-wrapping station," Mr. Mac was saying. "Plus, you'll be singing around dinnertime, so I'm sure there will be a big crowd."

"Big crowd—or captive audience?" Jacob said under his breath. Riley bit the inside of her cheek so she wouldn't crack up.

"Remember to tell your friends and family—

and don't forget your festive wear!" Mr. Mac said. "Good work today, everybody. See you at the mall on Wednesday. Riley and Jacob—you two seem to have an awful lot of spirit today, Christmas or otherwise. Would you please gather everyone's choir folders?"

"So, Riley, is your *festive wear* all ready?" asked Jacob as they started stacking the choir folders, which were filled with sheet music.

"Are you kidding? I've been ready for *months*," Riley joked. "I've got my Christmas-light necklace with *three* different flash settings; I've got my ornament earrings; I've got my Santa hat. Don't try to compete. You can't."

"Well, obviously," Jacob replied. "But my ugly Christmas sweater is pretty great. It has Rudolph the Red-Nosed Reindeer, and his nose lights up."

"Not bad, not bad," Riley said. "I don't have a Christmas sweater, actually—"

Riley didn't have a chance to finish her sentence, because the next thing she knew, Jacob was pretending to stagger backward. "*You* don't have a *Christmas* sweater?" he gasped. "What are you trying to do? Ruin Christmas and drag 3C down with you?"

"Hey!" Riley protested. "I will be *plenty* festive. You have *nothing* to worry about. I have, like, eight different Christmas accessories I can wear."

"Good. You had me worried for a minute," Jacob said, shaking his head. "No Christmas sweater. That's just crazy."

"What's crazy is that you seem to doubt I will be bringing the festive on Wednesday," Riley shot back with a grin. "Because believe me—I will."

"No doubt here," Jacob said. "I was just making sure. It's pretty festive at the food court. There's a lot of competition—that's all I'm saying."

A mischievous smile flickered across Riley's face. "Bring it on!" she replied.

When Riley got home from school, Theo was ready to pounce.

"When do we start making the ornaments?" Theo asked before Riley even had a chance to take her coat off. He was so excited that his voice got louder with every word.

"Soon," Riley promised, laughing. "Why don't you get out all the supplies? I'll get some Christmas music going."

"And I'll make some hot chocolate," Mom called from the kitchen. "It will be ornament central here in no time!"

The warmth of happiness filled Riley as she scrolled through the Christmas carol playlist. It got longer every year as the Archers added more songs to it, but Riley loved each and every one—even the goofy ones sung by cartoon characters. That was one of the things she loved most about her family's Christmas traditions. In some ways, they stayed the same from year to year...but they also grew and changed, just like the Archer family.

Crash!

Riley jumped as the loud noise jolted her out of her thoughts. She spun around just in time to see Theo, sprawled in the middle of the biggest mess Riley had ever seen!

"Theo!" Riley shrieked. "Are you okay? What happened?"

"I'm fine," Theo said. "You said to get the craft supplies. But I couldn't see where I was going and I think I walked into the chair."

"I didn't mean you had to bring them all at once!" Riley replied. Now that she knew for sure that Theo wasn't hurt, she had to smile. Theo was only six years old, but he'd tried to carry five big boxes at once—something even Riley couldn't manage.

"Come on, let's pick all this stuff up," Riley continued. "And look on the bright side—if we see anything we need for our ornaments, we can grab it now."

Theo looked worried. "Pick it *all* up?" he asked. "That's going to take forever! What if we run out of time to make ornaments?"

"Well, you'd better stop complaining and start cleaning so that doesn't happen!" Riley teased Theo as she handed him a big empty box. Theo got the message and started scooping up huge armfuls of craft supplies: felt and sequins and markers and yarn and pipe cleaners. He was like a human steam shovel!

"Hmm," Mom said as she came in and observed.

"Theo, I didn't know you could pick up so fast. This new skill is going to make a big difference the next time you have to clean your room."

"The difference is that he's super motivated now, Mom," Riley joked. "And so am I! I've got to get *two* ornaments done today. The clock is ticking!"

"How come two ornaments?" Theo asked.

"I'm going to give one to my Secret Snowflake at school—remember?" Riley reminded him. She rummaged through the mess to pluck two sheets of white felt and a packet of shimmery, rainbow-colored sequins from the pile.

"I guess," Theo said as he dumped an armful of supplies onto the table. "How come Secret Snowflake is all you talk about?"

"It's not *all* I talk about," Riley protested. "It's just on my mind a lot. Mrs. Darlington said that Secret Snowflake is a chance to be the best friend you can be to someone else. And that's important to me."

"Well said, Riley," Mom spoke up. "As long as it's not distracting you from your schoolwork, I think it's great."

Riley giggled. "But Mom—Secret Snowflake *is* my schoolwork!" she exclaimed.

"Your *other* schoolwork, then," Mom replied.

"Don't worry, Mom," Riley said. "It's all under control."

Soon the mess was almost cleaned up, but not because Riley and Theo had repacked all the boxes. Instead, they had picked out so many supplies that they'd basically transferred the mess to the dining room table instead!

Riley stared at her pile of supplies and started thinking about how she would transform them into an ornament. She'd been imagining a felt snowman ornament for weeks, with shiny sequin buttons, a festive cluster of holly on his fancy top hat, and a mug of cocoa in his mitten-covered hand. It would be totally adorable—and look great on her family's Christmas tree.

But what about Marcus? Would he want a cute, merry snowman ornament for his tree?

Suddenly, Riley wasn't so sure. And Sophia's words rang through her memory: "Boys are weird. Who knows what they like?"

A frown flitted across Riley's face. Not everyone was into Christmas as much as she was...and that was fine. Whatever. After all, the goal of Secret Snowflake was to be an awesome friend...which meant giving gifts someone else would want to receive, not gifts that *she* would want.

Riley sighed as she put the felt down.

"What's wrong?" asked Mom.

"I'm not sure I should make an ornament for Marcus," Riley admitted. "What if he thinks it's dumb? Or babyish?"

Theo's mouth dropped open. "Dumb? *Babyish?*" he exclaimed. "Christmas isn't dumb or babyish! Come on!"

"Yeah, but Marcus might think a snowman ornament is," Riley pointed out.

"Then he sounds like a jerk," Theo declared.

"Theo! Watch it," Mom said. "That's not a kind word to use." Then she turned to Riley. "Is there a way you could make a special ornament just for Marcus?" she asked. "Maybe something a little different from the one you make for our tree?"

Riley stared into space, deep in thought. What

kind of ornament *would* Marcus like? He was really into sports—everyone knew that—but she'd already given him something with a soccer ball, so that was out. What else?

"Football, surfing, skateboarding," Riley said under her breath...but none of them seemed very Christmasy. "Tennis, ski—yes! Skiing!"

"Huh?" asked Theo.

"I'll make a regular snowman ornament for us—and a skiing snowman for Marcus!" Riley exclaimed, the words tumbling out in a rush. "He loves sports, all sports, and I think he's totally into winter sports right now, because of course he is—it's winter! I'll make this skiing snowman with little skis out of Popsicle sticks, and poles out of pipe cleaners, and everything!"

"It sounds perfect," Mom said. "Go for it!"

Riley didn't need to be told twice. She was so inspired by her skiing snowman idea that she decided to make Marcus's ornament before the one for her family's tree. Using a fabric pen, Riley sketched a snowman shape on the white felt. Then she used her sharpest scissors to cut it out. Her thoughts drifted as she worked to what Sophia had said. By now, though, Riley was convinced that Sophia was wrong. There was no reason to assume Marcus wouldn't like a funny snowman ornament that reflected one of his favorite things to do. Sure, some people at school liked to act cooler than everybody else—but Marcus wasn't one of them; Riley was sure of it.

After all, there was a really good chance he'd chosen her name for Secret Snowflake, which meant that he was probably the one who wrote that poem for her. Anybody who would take the time to write a special poem for her Secret Snowflake gift clearly cared about Christmas as much as Riley did.

Tapping her fabric pen against the table, Riley thought about it. And the more she thought about it, the more certain she was that Marcus was her Secret Snowflake. He had to be... Who else could it possibly be? Who else in their class could write a poem like that?

Thoughts of the poem sparked a new idea in

Riley's mind. *What if I make a book of Christmas poems and quotes for Marcus?* she thought. *I could look them up on the Internet and copy them over in my best handwriting, onto that really special rice paper Aunt Cheryl gave me for my birthday. It could be a book all about the spirit of Christmas. About everything that makes Christmas special. Marcus would definitely appreciate that, and it would show him how special he is and how much I appreciated his poem.*

Riley was certain—she loved the idea. A hand-made book of Christmas poems would be the perfect last gift for Secret Snowflake. Which meant it would be perfect for Marcus!

Feeling energized and more excited than ever, Riley finished her work on Marcus's ornament, and by the time she was done, she had to admit that it might just be the best ornament she'd ever made! She'd created the snowman's face out of little bits of felt and even added red stripes to his blue felt scarf to match the design Marcus had made on his snowflake. The Popsicle-stick skis had turned out great, and after several tries she'd managed to create perfect poles that tucked snugly inside the snowman's little gloved hands. Riley was bursting with pride over the ornament—she just hoped she got to see Marcus's face when he opened it!

The next morning, Riley made her second stealthy Secret Snowflake delivery. It was just as easy as the first one—and just as thrilling, too. *By the time Secret Snowflake is over, I'll be like a top spy,* Riley thought with a grin. Just as quickly, though, she pushed the thought out of her mind. She didn't want to think about Secret Snowflake ending, even if it did mean a big party *and* all the answers revealed. Riley was having way too much fun.

Out of habit, Riley peeked into her own snowflake mailbox—but it was empty. She wasn't worried, though. Once again, she'd arrived at school earlier than most of her classmates, and besides, she'd already received one perfect present. Was it too much to hope for that her Secret Snowflake would bring her another gift today?

She went back to her seat to wait, drumming her fingers impatiently on the scratched desktop. One by one, the other students began to fill the classroom. Riley glanced up every time she heard someone in the doorway.

But Marcus still hadn't arrived.

Riley watched Alice enter the room, walking with her head down. She tucked her backpack under her seat, then glanced over at the Secret Snowflake mailboxes. Then the weirdest thing happened: Alice didn't even bother to check her mailbox.

Riley frowned a little. *Isn't she curious?* she wondered. *I mean, I check my Secret Snowflake mailbox, like, three times a day.*

But maybe Riley was so excited to check her mailbox because she had an awesome Secret Snowflake. Her frown deepened. *Has Sophia even figured out Alice's first present?* she thought. If not, Sophia would have to come up with something soon. There were only eight more days of Secret Snowflake until the big reveal. There was no set number of presents your Secret Snowflake *had* to give you, but going the first two days without receiving a present seemed like a long time to Riley.

There was something else going on, though. Alice wasn't just acting like someone who hadn't received a gift yet. She was acting like someone who didn't expect to ever receive one.

I'll ask Sophia when she gets here, Riley thought. *If she still has no clue, I'll help her make a present. We'll figure something out.*

The moment Sophia got to class, though, she made a beeline for her Secret Snowflake mailbox. Her excited shriek told Riley that Sophia had been snowflaked! Riley stood up, craning her neck to try to see. She didn't want to rush in and crowd Sophia while she was still opening her present—but it turned out that Riley didn't need to worry about that. Sophia practically raced back to Riley's desk before she'd even opened her gift. In that moment, Riley decided to ask Sophia about Alice later. She didn't want to dampen Sophia's excitement over her first Secret Snowflake present.

"Riley! Look!" Sophia exclaimed. "I got a Secret Snowflake delivery!"

"Yeah, I had a feeling that was what happened," Riley teased her friend. "What are you waiting for—open it! I can't wait to see what's inside!"

"Neither can I!" Sophia squealed. She turned the envelope over in her hand and tore a ragged hole along the side. In her excitement, Sophia tried to dump the contents in her palm—but instead they fell all over Riley's desk! A swirling cloud of sparkling confetti spilled from the envelope and made an avalanche that tumbled into the aisle—and even onto Marcus's chair!

"Oh no!" Sophia and Riley cried as the warning bell rang. They'd made a massive Secret Snowflake mess—and class was about to start. Mrs. Darlington would *not* be happy...and Riley had a feeling that Marcus wouldn't be amused to find his chair coated in confetti and glitter, either.

Riley dropped to her knees and started to sweep the confetti into a pile with her hands. "Come on, we have to clean this up before—" she began.

But Sophia just stood there, looking dreamy. "It's a gift card to the candy store in the mall," she said. "You know the one where you can mix and match *any* candy you want? With the gigantic lollipops in the window?"

"Of course I know it," Riley replied. "You had your seventh birthday party there, remember? Let's hurry, Marcus is probably—"

"Probably what?" a new voice said.

Riley glanced up—right into Marcus's face!

"We had a . . . confetti accident," Riley said. She immediately stifled a groan. What a dumb thing to say!

But Marcus, amazingly, didn't seem to think so. He laughed—and not at Riley. "Looks pretty bad," he said. "A real confetti pileup. Was it hazardous conditions?"

"Oh yeah," Riley said, playing along. "Really hazardous. The roads were covered in . . . glitter."

Marcus chuckled as he shook his head and swept the confetti from his chair onto the floor. Then he sat down and pulled a comic book out of his backpack.

Riley continued picking up the pieces of confetti from the floor around Marcus's desk. *Why is he just sitting down?* she wondered. *Doesn't he want to check his Secret Snowflake mailbox? Everybody else checks it the second they get to school! Did the confetti distract him? Did he forget?*

"Here, Riley—let me do that," Sophia said as she knelt next to her friend. "You don't have to clean up my Secret Snowflake mess."

"I don't mind," Riley said automatically. She tried to radio Marcus with her mind: *Check your mailbox. Check your mailbox. Check your mailbox.*

But he didn't budge.

"I hope my Secret Snowflake doesn't feel bad about the mess," Sophia was saying. "I'd feel totally bad, if it was me. But it's not like they can just come help clean it up with us....I mean, that would be totally obvious....I know *I* would be worried I'd give it away!"

"Hmm, yes," Riley replied. "It *is* very surprising that we're not being mobbed with offers of help. I know *everyone* likes cleaning stuff up off the floor."

"You know what I mean!" Sophia said, laughing. "Anyway, listen, we *have* to go to the mall, because I can't wait to use my gift card at the Candy Emporium...."

Sophia was still talking, but Riley's thoughts had drifted off in a totally different direction. She was already going to the mall for 3C—and Marcus was sitting right there in front of her—

"I have an idea," Riley said loudly. "I'll be at the mall tomorrow afternoon for the 3C concert. You should totally come! It starts at five o'clock—in the plaza near the food court."

"You guys are singing at the mall?" Sophia asked. "Really?"

"Yeah, it's kind of a 3C tradition," Riley said. "It's *really* fun. Better than you can imagine! And we can hit the candy store afterward. Maybe you could even come over for dinner that night."

"Cool. I'll be there," Sophia promised.

"Austin!" Marcus called out suddenly as one of his buddies entered the classroom. "Why are you wearing that ugly shirt again, man? Do you need me to buy you a new one?"

Riley glanced at the back of Marcus's head. He was definitely sitting close enough to overhear every word she'd said about the mall. She was sure of it.

Now she just had to wait and see if Marcus would come to the concert.

Chapter 6

Riley tugged at the sleeves of her sweater. She'd stayed up late the night before adding loops of gold tinsel to the neckline and each cuff—*not* because Jacob had joked that her 3C outfit might not be festive enough, but because Riley had decided that it never hurt to add a little more sparkle at Christmastime. She wanted to look her best for the 3C concert—especially if Marcus showed up! And Riley was really happy with her outfit—from her plaid skirt to her red sweater to her Santa hat to the best addition of all: a Christmas tree pin with blinking, rainbow-colored lights that had been left in her Secret Snowflake mailbox that morning!

Riley stood at the entrance to the food court and looked around for anyone she knew. The area seemed more crowded than usual, and not just with all the extra shoppers who were stocking up on Christmas presents. A cozy little cottage—Santa's Workshop—had been constructed nearby, with the mall Santa sitting on a large green velvet chair. A line of cranky kids—who, coincidentally, were also decked out in their finest festive wear—and their tired parents looped all the way to the parking lot!

That wasn't all, Riley noticed. A table near the sandwich place had been transformed into a gift-wrapping station, complete with another long line. The *rrrrip* of scissors slicing through rolls of bright wrapping paper could be heard over all the other noise.

Well, Mr. Mac was right, I guess, Riley thought. *We'll have a big audience tonight. And I guess Jacob was right, too, because I don't think most of them will be at the 3C concert by choice!*

Even though Riley had just arrived at the mall, she was already starting to regret her late-night crafting spree. The tinsel trim was a lot itchier now that she'd been wearing it for several minutes than it had been when she'd tried on her sweater last night.

Riley rubbed her itchy wrist, then glanced at her watch. She still didn't see anyone from school, which made Riley wonder if maybe she had enough time to dash into one of the stores and ask to borrow their scissors. Then she could cut off all this scratchy tinsel and—

"Riley! Over here!" Mr. Mac called.

Riley's heart sank, though she tried to smile. Just past Mr. Mac, she could see that almost everybody else was assembled. It looked like he was about to start warm-ups. She'd be stuck wearing scratchy tinsel for the entire performance.

At least Riley wasn't the only one all decked out in her festive Christmas best. Pretty much everyone had a Santa hat, except the eighth graders, who were all wearing reindeer antlers instead. Riley wondered for a second if that's what they'd been whispering about at 3C practice the other day. One of the boys in sixth grade was even wearing a light-up tie in the shape of a Christmas tree!

Riley hurried over to the group and took her place next to Jacob. He mumbled something under his breath.

"What?" she whispered.

"Nice pin," he replied. "Is it new?"

"Yeah, thanks—I have a pretty great Secret Snowflake," she replied.

Mr. Mac started playing the scales on his electric keyboard so the kids could warm up their voices before the performance began. Riley shifted a little and tugged at her collar, all the while keeping an eye out for Marcus. The warm-ups were in a side hallway that led to a parking lot. She didn't have a clear view of the food court. Maybe Marcus and his friends had grabbed some pizza and were hanging out before the concert started.

Mr. Mac looked pleased at the end of the warm-up. "That sounded great—just great," he said. "If you sing that well when we perform, the crowd will go wild! Now, we set up some risers between

Santa's Workshop and the gift-wrapping station, so let's just make our way over there and get this show on the road."

Mr. Mac had always coached the members of 3C that the performance began not when they started to sing—but when the audience first caught a glimpse of them. Riley put on her brightest smile as the choir members filed out of the hallway, toward the risers.

"Oh! Miss!" a voice suddenly called out.

Riley glanced around. *Is she talking to me?* Riley wondered.

Sure enough, a woman was approaching her. "Thank goodness you're here. I've been waiting for more than *ten minutes* to have my gifts wrapped!" she said. "I simply cannot understand why the mall would understaff the gift-wrapping station this close to Christmas!"

The lady thrust an armful of shopping bags at Riley and waited expectantly. It took Riley a moment to understand. "Oh! I'm sorry—I'm not a gift-wrapper," she explained as she tried to return the packages. "I'm here to sing."

"Sing?" the woman repeated, looking confused. "We don't need singing—we need gift-wrapping!"

"I—I can't help you," Riley stammered.

"Young lady, where is your manager?" the woman said sternly. "You are wearing the same Santa hats as the other gift-wrappers, and I think your manager would be very interested to know that you're not willing to help a customer."

"Come on, Riley," Jacob said loudly. "Don't want to miss your solo!"

Riley flashed him a grateful smile. She didn't even have a solo, but he had given her the perfect opportunity to sidle away from the frustrated woman.

"Thanks," Riley said under her breath.

"Don't worry about it," Jacob told her. "When I got here, some lady thought I was working at the Santa photos. She wanted me to throw away her kid's dirty diaper!"

"Gross," Riley said, shuddering. "We might need to rethink wearing such festive outfits to the mall. It's just too confusing for all the frazzled shoppers."

"No kidding." Jacob chuckled. "We'd better start singing stat—before they start a shopping riot or something."

"You know what they say," Riley joked, "music has charms to soothe the savage beast."

"And there's no beast more savage than a Christmas shopper in the mall jungle," Jacob said. His voice got all serious, like an announcer for a wildlife documentary. "Experts advise that you avoid disturbing the Christmas shopper in the wilderness of the shopping mall, where they are at their most ruthless and cunning."

"Quit it!" Riley whispered through her laughter. "You're going to make me laugh through the songs!"

Jacob's eyes were twinkling as he pretended to lock his mouth shut, then toss the imaginary key over this shoulder. 3C's steps made the metal risers clang as they filed into their places. Riley scanned the crowd and noticed several people she knew. Her little brother, Theo, was waving wildly from the front row—as if Riley could've missed spotting him! And Sophia was sitting next to him, subtly holding up her gift card to the Candy Emporium while giving Riley a thumbs-up. Becca and Marian from school were in the audience, too, and even shy, quiet Alice was sitting off to the side, all by herself.

What about Marcus, though? Was he there?

If the plaza had been less crowded, Riley would've known for sure. But there were so many people—and so many packages—and so many lines snaking back and forth, lines for gift-wrapping and lines for visiting Santa and lines for the food court....

Riley caught a flash of red hair, and her heartbeat quickened. Was that Marcus? Maybe he had arrived just in time!

She craned her neck, focusing her eyes on the back of the crowd, staring so intently that she didn't notice that Mr. Mac had raised his hands to start conducting.

Suddenly, Riley was surrounded by song. The beautiful voices of her friends in 3C spiraled into the air, performing just how they had rehearsed—except for Riley. She alone wasn't singing.

Riley jolted back to the present, blushing as red

as her Santa hat. She couldn't *believe* she'd missed the cue for their first song—and all because she was trying to find her crush in the crowd! Riley flipped open her choir folder and forced herself to focus, pushing all thoughts of Marcus from her mind. Then she joined in the song, which made it easier than she expected to forget about Marcus.

The live Christmas music worked its magic, even in a place as unmagical as the Hampton Creek Mall. Riley could see it from the risers—the way the stress in people's faces softened; the way their feet tapped in time to the songs, and their heads bobbed along to the music. She wouldn't be a bit surprised if some of them were humming along to the familiar tunes.

Mr. Mac definitely knew what he was doing when he picked the songs for 3C's program at the mall. Almost all of his selections were upbeat and catchy, building to a fun, jazzy rendition of "Jingle Bells" for their big finale. When Riley heard Mr. Mac play the intro on his keyboard, her heart felt bigger, as if it were inflating with happiness. She would make up for her late cue; she would pour all her heart and soul into singing for this audience, these Christmas shoppers—and by doing so, Riley would be spreading the Christmas spirit that made the holiday season so magical for her. Mr. Mac always encouraged the kids to rock out during this song, and maybe Riley would go for it! Maybe—

BEEP! BEEP! BEEP! BEEP!

The sound was so shrill, so piercing, that Riley plugged her fingers in her ears and winced with pain. Mr. Mac stopped playing abruptly. What was the point? No one could hear him over the blaring alarm.

An uneasy murmur arose from the crowd. Riley looked around, unsure. What was going on?

"I don't know about you, but those aren't exactly the jingle bells I was imagining," Jacob cracked.

Before Riley could reply, the loudspeakers crackled overhead, and a voice said, "Attention, shoppers. Please stay calm and proceed to the nearest exit."

Riley sniffed the air nervously. Was that smoke

she smelled—or was it just her imagination? She glanced over to the food court and gasped.

Smoke was billowing out of the burger place!

"Look!" Riley cried, grabbing Jacob's elbow.

Whoooooshhshhhshhhshhhhh!

An assistant manager ran over to the deep fryer and hosed it down with a fire extinguisher. A massive white cloud consumed the smoking equipment until Riley couldn't see if it was still on fire. The problem must've been under control, though, because people in the food court started to applaud.

"Guess I won't be having my extra-crispy fries after all," Jacob said near Riley's ear.

She laughed, then realized she was still holding on to his elbow. Riley dropped her hand faster than if she'd touched something on fire. "That was freaky," she said. "I've never seen a real fire before."

"That's what happens when good fries go bad," Jacob joked. "We should probably have a moment of silence for all the fries we lost today."

"Proceed to the nearest exit," the voice blared over the loudspeaker.

Mr. Mac rubbed his chin. "You heard the lady," he announced. "Come on, 3C—let's go. No running, no pushing, no panicking."

"But the fire's over," one of the eighth graders said. "Can't we finish our show?"

"They're still evacuating, probably as a precaution," Mr. Mac replied. "Think of it like a fire drill at school—and a great story you can tell all your friends tomorrow!"

Riley smiled ruefully as she tugged at her itchy tinsel trim. She had a feeling that she'd be telling stories about the Hampton Creek Mall concert— in all its disastrous glory—for a *long* time to come.

That night, Sophia came over for dinner after their shopping spree at the Candy Emporium. She and Riley couldn't stop giggling about all the things that went wrong during 3C's performance. Whenever they started to settle down, one of them whispered, "Smokin'!" and they cracked up again. Then Sophia grew serious.

"Are you okay?" Sophia asked.

"What do you mean?" asked Riley. "I know it wasn't the greatest choral performance I've ever done, but I don't think we need to print up 'I Survived 3C at Hampton Creek Mall' shirts or anything."

"No, your neck," Sophia said. "It's kind of pink. Like you have a rash or something."

Riley stood up so she could glance at her reflection in the mirror over her dresser. Sure enough, she had a pink ring circling her neck—and a matching one on each wrist. "Just my luck—I must have a tinsel allergy!" she groaned.

"Well, on the plus side, your sweater looked awesome," Sophia said.

"I can't believe I missed my cue for the opening song," Riley said, shaking her head. "Are you sure you didn't notice? It must have been so obvious."

"You know I would tell you if I noticed," Sophia assured her. "Trust me—you were totally cool about it. Very subtle. No one suspected a thing."

"I hope you're right," Riley replied. "Maybe it's best that Marcus didn't show up. I probably would've died of embarrassment if he'd seen me mess up like that."

Sophia looked surprised. "You were expecting Marcus?" she asked in astonishment. "Did you, like, *invite* him?"

"No, of course not!" Riley said. "I just, you know, talked about the concert really loud when he was nearby."

Sophia had a mischievous look in her eyes. "Smokin'!" she replied.

"Stop! I can't breathe!" Riley complained as she cracked up again.

"Seriously, though, that was pretty smooth—telling Marcus about the concert without, you know, *telling* him about the concert," Sophia said.

"I tried to be subtle," Riley explained. "But maybe I was too subtle. It was cool that some people from school came—you were there, and I saw those twins from eighth grade, and Alice...."

Riley's voice trailed off unexpectedly.

"What?" Sophia prompted her.

"Alice," Riley repeated. "I just realized...*Alice* was there."

"And...?" Sophia said.

"Well, doesn't that—surprise you a little?" Riley said. "She always keeps to herself; she never talks to anybody. But now I'm wondering if she overheard me talking about the 3C concert...and I mentioned it was at the mall...."

"Still not following," Sophia told her.

"Maybe she doesn't know where to go...or what to do...or who to hang out with," Riley said. "Maybe she's been feeling totally clueless. If she really is super shy, she might not know how to make friends."

A troubled expression crossed Sophia's face. "I never thought about it like that," she said. "I always assumed she didn't want to hang out. I mean, she never talks to anybody...or even smiles...."

"I probably wouldn't smile, either, if I didn't know anything about my new town or the kids at my new school," Riley pointed out.

"Stop!" Sophia said, covering her face with her hair. "You're making me feel really bad."

"We should all feel really bad," Riley said. "Seventh grade has been crazy so far and none of us have gone out of our way to get to know her . . . but that's no excuse. Have you made any Secret Snowflake deliveries to Alice's mailbox yet?"

"No," Sophia admitted.

For a moment, neither girl said anything.

"I think I know how we can fix this," Riley finally said.

"How?" asked Sophia.

"Secret Snowflake!" Riley exclaimed.

"You are Secret Snowflake obsessed!" Sophia laughed. "I'm not sure it's the answer to *every* problem, though. Like, just because I start leaving presents for Alice won't solve the fact that she hasn't made any friends here."

"No—you're right. But it's a start," Riley said. "Remember how you didn't know what to do for Alice because you don't know her?"

"Yeah. That's still my problem," Sophia said.

"Well, why don't you use the Secret Snowflake gifts to show Alice how awesome it is to live in Hampton Creek?" Riley said, getting more excited with every word. "You might not know Alice very well, but you know *everything* about Hampton

Creek. You could give her a map of the town with all the cool places to hang out marked on it...a pretty bookmark and an application for a library card...a roll of tokens for the arcade...."

Sophia clapped her hands together. "Riley! You're a genius!" she gushed. "The Secret Snowflake gifts could be like a scavenger hunt that leads her all over Hampton Creek so she can start to feel at home!"

"Exactly!" Riley cried. "And that's just the start. I'm going to invite her to join 3C. I mean, she showed up to the concert. Maybe she's interested!"

"And I'm going to invite her to hang out at my house over Christmas break," Sophia declared. "But not until the end of Secret Snowflake. I don't want her to guess my identity just yet."

"Ooh! What if we invite Alice to a slumber party?" Riley suggested.

"I'll ask my mom—but I know she'll say yes," Sophia replied, grinning. "Maybe we could do it on New Year's Eve! We could stay up until midnight—"

"*Way* past midnight!" Riley chimed in.

"And get a bunch of noisemakers and sparkle confetti—"

"You mean you haven't had *enough* sparkle confetti already?" Riley joked.

"You can never have too much sparkle confetti," Sophia declared.

"I guess you're right when it comes to New Year's Eve," Riley replied with a grin. "Just when I thought December couldn't get more exciting, now we have a Secret Snowflake sleepover to plan!"

Chapter 7

Riley reached into her pocket and wrapped her fingers around her latest Secret Snowflake surprise— a small bottle of beautiful, bright blue nail polish. It wasn't just her favorite color; it was pretty much her favorite shade of her favorite color, and Riley couldn't *wait* to get home and do her nails. She'd almost been tempted to break it out during lunch and paint her pinky nail—just to see how it would shimmer with all those specks of sparkly glitter—but had managed to resist. The cafeteria monitor's strictness was legendary, and Riley knew she'd be crushed if her gorgeous new nail polish was confiscated.

Not too much longer, Riley promised herself. After all, school was over for the day. She just had 3C rehearsal left—and then she could give herself the most sparkly manicure ever!

More than that, though, Riley was excited to see if Alice would show up for 3C rehearsal. She'd seemed surprised when Riley came up to her in homeroom to thank her for coming to the 3C concert—and even more surprised when Riley invited her to join 3C. There were just two concerts left, but if Alice showed up at rehearsal on Friday, Riley had a feeling Mr. Macintosh would let her join.

When Riley arrived at the music room, she was surprised to see that Mr. Mac wasn't there yet. She wandered over to Jacob, who was staring at a half-assembled, metallic silver Christmas tree in the middle of the floor.

"What is *that*?" Riley asked.

"Space Christmas," Jacob said in a robotic voice. "Alien Tree. Prepare for blastoff."

Riley giggled. "I've never seen such a weird tree," she said. "Is it made of metal?"

Jacob reached down to touch it. "It's not sharp," he said. "It's almost like the branches are made of metallic pipe cleaners. Seems kind of old, huh? Like one of those retro-futuristic decorations from the nineteen-fifties."

"Where's Mr. Mac?" Riley asked, glancing around the room.

"Not sure," Jacob replied. "But his coffee is on the desk, so he can't be too far. Maybe ten feet away, at the most."

Riley giggled. It was no secret that Mr. Mac was practically addicted to coffee. He even had his very own personal coffeepot in the music room. Sometimes when Riley arrived at the music room, the smell of freshly brewed coffee filled the air, and Mr. Mac joked that they'd be rehearsing in his acoustic cafe!

"So…" Jacob said in a funny voice that sounded a little higher than usual. "Still getting good stuff from your Secret Snowflake?"

"Oh yeah, definitely!" Riley replied. "In fact, today I got—"

"Hey—some help here!" Mr. Mac called as he lugged a massive box through the doorway. Riley and Jacob hurried over to help.

"What's with the tree?" Jacob asked.

"And what's in the box?" Riley added. It was way too heavy to be sheet music.

"You'll see," Mr. Mac said mysteriously. He clapped his hands together. "Okay, people, let's get—"

His voice broke off unexpectedly. Riley glanced around the room curiously—and spotted Alice and Sophia standing by the door!

"Hi, girls. Are you here for 3C rehearsal?" Mr. Mac asked.

"Yeah. Is it too late to join this year?" asked Sophia.

"Definitely not," Mr. Mac said, beaming. "Riley, grab some extra music, okay?"

Riley grinned as she hurried over to get some sheet music for Alice and Sophia, then crossed the room to the doorway. "You came!" she whispered to Alice. "Yay!"

Then Riley turned to Sophia. "And so did you!"

Sophia shrugged. "After the way you talked it up, I had to check it out for myself," she replied. But Riley could tell she was just trying to act cool.

"Well, I'm glad you did," Riley replied. "I think you're gonna love it!"

When everyone was settled, Mr. Mac patted the large cardboard box. "Can anyone guess what's in here?" he asked.

"Is it new music?" someone called out.

"A tuba?" joked one of the boys, making everyone laugh.

"Not exactly," Mr. Mac replied. Then he opened the flaps of the box to reveal a massive jumble of tinsel garlands, brightly colored baubles, strands of twinkle lights, and more.

"Christmas decorations!" he continued. "This is actually just one of *ten boxes* that belonged to my grandmother. She died last year, at the impressive age of ninety-nine. Ninety-nine years old! And for her entire life, she loved Christmas more than anything. I don't know, maybe it's genetic."

"It's definitely genetic," Jacob whispered to Riley.

"So I have all these decorations that used to

belong to her," Mr. Mac continued. "Way more than I need for my apartment. So I've been wondering, what should I do with them? And after our concert at the Hampton Creek Mall, I finally figured it out."

Lillian's hand shot into the air. "Are we going to decorate the music room?" she asked.

"Yes!" Mr. Mac replied. "Starting with my grandma's old tree. I figured we need a place to put the last Secret Snowflake presents at the party. And I think you'll be working on something in art class that we can use to decorate the room, too. I have a feeling this year's Christmas party and Secret Snowflake reveal is going to be the best one yet.

"But I'm getting ahead of myself," Mr. Mac continued. "Anyway, I have way too many decorations to use just in the music room. Anyone else want to guess what we're going to do with them?"

"We could decorate the whole school," Ben suggested.

"Getting warmer," Mr. Mac told him. "Think even bigger than that."

Riley tapped her fingers against the bottle of polish in her pocket. If it was a bigger deal than decorating the whole school…

She raised her hand. "Are they for our next concert?"

"We have a winner!" Mr. Mac announced. "Heads up!"

In a blink, Mr. Mac reached into the box, then pitched a lightweight ornament made of ribbons in Riley's direction. She caught it right before it sailed past her head.

"Good eye!" Jacob said.

Riley grinned at him. "Thanks!"

"As you know, our next performance will be at the Sunny Acres Retirement Community," Mr. Mac explained. "Which is a fancy way of saying 'nursing home.' And this time, we're going to do more than just sing."

"Will we have another fire drill, too?" Jacob joked.

Mr. Mac shook his head. "I sure hope not," he replied. "But I was thinking it would be nice to step it up a little. Not *just* show up and sing, but make ourselves useful, too. I mean, can you think of a better way to spread Christmas cheer than doing good deeds?"

"No," everyone chorused.

"Neither can I," Mr. Mac said. "That's why I called Sunny Acres and asked if we could decorate the common room for Christmas. And they said yes!"

The kids broke out into spontaneous cheers. Riley thought this was an amazing idea and was happy to see that her fellow 3Cers agreed.

"And that's not all," Mr. Mac said after they'd quieted down. "I'd like to challenge all of you—every single member of 3C—to think of something special *you* can do for the residents at Sunny Acres, too. How can you make their holiday happier? How might you bring them comfort and joy?"

There was a pause.

"Don't everybody talk all at once." Mr. Mac broke the silence with a joke, and everyone laughed. Riley had to wonder if everyone else felt the same way she did—already dreaming up ways in which they would rise to the challenge.

"Partner up! Make it fun!" Mr. Mac encouraged them. "You can even work together over the weekend. I can't wait to see what you'll come up with. Now, give me five minutes to get our new members up to speed. Try to keep it down to a dull roar, okay? Alice and Sophia, would you come here for a moment?"

Before she left, Sophia tugged on Riley's sleeve. "We'll partner up, all three of us," she said. "You, me, and Alice."

"Of course," Riley agreed.

In a split second, though, she remembered something: Jacob was the only other seventh grader in 3C—until about five minutes ago. If Sophia and Alice hadn't joined, Riley had a feeling that she and Jacob would've worked together on the surprise for Sunny Acres. She felt guilty for leaving him out in the cold just because her best friend had suddenly joined 3C.

She snuck a glance at Jacob out of the corner of her eye. He wasn't goofing around for a change; instead, he was staring at his sheet music like he was studying it. Riley could tell that he'd heard every word of her exchange with Sophia.

"Hey," Riley began.

Jacob looked up. She hadn't really noticed his eyes before—they weren't just brown but flecked with green and gold. *Hazel* was the word that popped into Riley's brain before she focused on what she really wanted to say.

"You want to partner for this?" Riley asked. Did her voice sound weird? She couldn't tell. Besides, why should it? Jacob was a friend, just like Sophia. "I think Sophia and Alice are going to come over this weekend. We could all figure out something to do together. If you want."

A slow smile spread across Jacob's face. "Sure. Sounds cool," he said.

"Cool," Riley repeated. "I'll text you later."

After a flurry of group texts, Riley, Sophia, Alice, and Jacob decided to meet up at Riley's house on Sunday afternoon for a Christmas cookie bake-off. Riley's mom took her to the grocery store so she could buy everything they'd need: flour, sugar, butter, eggs, and lots of chocolate chips, of course. The

Archer family had Christmas cookie recipes that had been passed down for generations.

Shortly before her friends arrived, Riley was busy arranging everything in the kitchen when she realized that Theo was hanging out near the chocolate chips— *too* near the chocolate chips. "Shoo," she said. "You know we need those for the cookies."

"Can't I just have a few?" Theo pleaded. "Just one little handful? Please?"

"No way," Riley said firmly. "If I open that bag now, we both know what will happen. You'll start eating them, and you won't stop, and then we might not have enough! Besides, these cookies aren't even for us; they're for the people who live at Sunny Acres. We're trying to make their Christmases better, not worse by delivering them sad cookies with barely any chocolate chips."

"But—" Theo protested.

Ding-dong!

Riley held up one finger. "Don't even think about it," she warned him. "If I come back and that bag is open, I *will* tell Mom."

Then Riley hurried to the door, trusting that

Theo would remember to be on his best behavior this close to Christmas. She swung it open to find Jacob standing on the doorstep.

"Merry Christmas cookies!" he said, holding up a bag from the grocery store. "I wasn't sure what kind we were making, so I got the basics—sugar, butter, that sort of thing."

"Hey, thanks!" Riley said. "You didn't have to do that. Come on in."

In the hallway, Jacob shrugged off his coat. "Where should I—" he began.

"I'll take it," Riley replied. While she hung up Jacob's coat, she kept talking. "I thought we could make a few different kinds of cookies. We have a *ton* of cookie cutters, like way more than any one family needs, but maybe that's good since we'll have cookie-baking teams today. I figured we could pick out some recipes once—"

Ding-dong!

"Everyone else gets here," Riley finished. She opened the front door again—and found Alice and Sophia standing on the front step.

"Perfect timing!" Riley exclaimed. "Jacob's already

here, and I don't know how much longer I can pro-
tect the chocolate chips from Theo, so we'd better
start baking immediately, if not sooner!"

"On it!" Sophia announced. She pushed past
Riley and Jacob and hollered, "Theo! Leave those
chocolate chips alone or you won't get *any* cookies,
I mean it!"

Jacob grimaced. "Is she, uh, always like that?" he
asked.

"It's a big joke around here," Riley assured him.
"Since Sophia has three little brothers, it's like she
can't turn off her big-sister voice. It just comes out
automatically. Theo doesn't even care—it cracks
him up."

Then Riley turned to Alice. "Do you have any
brothers or sisters?" she asked.

"I have a big sister, but she left for college last
August," Alice said. "A couple weeks before we
moved here."

"Oh," Riley said. "That must have been a lot to
deal with all at once, huh?"

Alice nodded. "Yeah, it was. But Claire is almost
done with her first semester—she's coming home

next week! She's never even seen our new house before. I mean, in pictures, yeah, but not in person."

"That's exciting!" Riley said. "I bet you can't wait to see her."

"I can't," Alice said—and then she smiled at Riley.

Theo poked his head out of the kitchen. "And *I* can't wait to eat *cookies*," he groaned as he flopped down to the floor. "Come on, Riley! Isn't it time to start baking yet?"

"Ignore him," Riley told Jacob and Alice. "He'll start acting like a civilized human being more quickly that way."

But Jacob had already walked over to Theo. "Theo, my man, you gotta get up," he said, holding out his hand. "These cookies aren't gonna bake themselves—and you can't exactly help if you're writhing around on the floor like a half-squashed caterpillar."

Theo clambered up at once. "Help? I can help?" he asked.

Riley shrugged. "If you want," she said. "But no

snacking on raw cookie dough! You don't want to get sick right before Christmas."

"But it's so yummy," Theo protested. "Cookie dough is my favorite."

"Mine too, but we're not supposed to eat it raw," Riley said. "Anyway, you can hold out until the cookies are fully baked. I know it."

In the kitchen, Riley pulled the special box of Christmas recipes off the shelf. "Take a look at these and let me know if anything sounds good," she said as she passed the recipe cards around to her friends. "I definitely think we should make sugar cookies. Then we can use the cookie cutters and decorate them with frosting and sprinkles. That's my favorite part!"

Alice rummaged around in her backpack and pulled out a set of small vials with different decorations in them—silvery snowflakes, tiny gold balls, a rainbow of sprinkles. She even had sugar-coated holly berries with bright green candy leaves. "I brought these, if you want to use them."

"Those are perfect!" Riley said. "Look at the snowflakes—they're so sparkly!"

"That's from the extra sugar on top," Alice said. "Which makes them extra yummy!"

"We're going to make chocolate chip cookies, though, aren't we?" Theo said anxiously. "I mean, that's why you bought all those bags of chocolate chips, right?"

"If everybody else wants to," Riley told him. She tried to give him a look, the same one Mom used that clearly meant *Watch it*, but Theo didn't seem to notice.

"What about these?" Jacob asked, holding up a recipe card that said "Buckeyes" at the top. "They sound amazing—and they're dipped in melted chocolate."

"Buckeyes?" Theo read. He glanced at Riley. "We've never made those before."

"Not for, like, six years, anyway," she replied, reaching out to tousle Theo's hair. "They've got peanut butter in them."

"Oh," Theo said, sounding disappointed.

"Theo's allergic to peanuts," Sophia explained to Alice and Jacob. "The Archer house is a peanut-free zone."

"Sorry," Jacob said. "I didn't realize."

"Don't worry about it," Riley assured him. "I fill up on peanut butter when I hang out at Sophia's."

"And luckily, I'm not allergic to chocolate!" Theo chimed in.

"That *is* lucky," Jacob replied.

"It can be kind of tricky sometimes, especially when we eat out," Riley said. "But some places don't use any peanuts, like Creekside Cafe & Chocolates, so when we go there, Theo can order anything off the menu."

"These snowball cookies look good," Alice spoke up.

"They taste good, too," Riley said. "I bet the people at Sunny Acres will love them."

"How about the candy-cane twists?" Sophia suggested. "You know those are my favorites!"

"That's why I bought peppermint extract at the grocery store!" Riley replied. "Okay, so we've got decorated sugar cookies, snowballs, candy-cane twists, and—"

"Please?" Theo said, hopping from one foot to the other. "Please, please, please, *please*?"

Riley's and Jacob's eyes met. "Chocolate chip cookies!" they announced at the same time.

Theo cheered and did a silly victory dance across the linoleum floor, which made everyone laugh.

"Okay, that's enough messing around," Riley finally said. "We've got *four* different kinds of cookies to make—and not a lot of time to get it all done. Let's break into teams."

"Team Snowball Cookie–slash–Candy-Cane Twist, reporting for duty," Sophia announced, linking arms with Alice.

"Awesome. Jacob, Theo, and I will make the sugar cookies and the chocolate chip cookies," Riley said. "On your mark, get set, *bake!*"

As the Christmas cookie bake-off got under way, Riley couldn't remember the last time she'd laughed so hard. Puffs of flour floated into the air, while spilled sugar crunched underfoot like frost. Riley had worried that Theo would be more of a hindrance than a helper, but it turned out he took the cookie baking really seriously. *I bet he likes hanging out with the "big kids,"* Riley thought, hiding her smile. And it didn't hurt that Jacob treated Theo like a real person, not a pest. It was funny how Theo seemed to already look up to Jacob, even though they'd just met.

The chocolate chip cookie dough was the easiest one to make, so they were ready to be baked before the others. "Mom!" Riley called. "A little help with the oven!"

"Be right there!" Mom called back.

Riley turned to her friends with an apologetic half shrug. "My mom still wants to supervise stuff like the oven," she said.

"Mine too!" Alice exclaimed. "I thought it was just me."

"Definitely not," Sophia assured her.

"Yeah, join the club," Jacob added.

"What club?" Mom asked as she entered the kitchen.

"The…Christmas Cookie Baking Club," Riley joked, exchanging a sly grin with her friends. Even Theo played along.

"Well, your club looks like it's thriving!" Mom said brightly. "What are you going to bake first?"

"Chocolate chip!" Theo crowed. He grabbed a

baking tray that was covered with twelve perfectly round scoops of cookie dough.

"Hang on there—that's my job," Mom said as she swooped in to take the tray.

"I already preheated the oven," Riley told her.

"Smart cookie," Mom replied with a wink, making Riley groan. Then Mom slid the tray into the oven while Riley set the timer for twelve minutes.

The delicious aroma of freshly baked cookies slowly filled the kitchen. Even Riley's mouth was watering, so she could hardly blame Theo for camping out right in front of the oven, watching the cookies bake through the glass door. When the timer finally went *ding!* everyone was ready for a cookie break.

By then, Theo was a little bored with baking. He took a plate with three cookies into the living room to watch a movie, while Riley and her friends worked on the trickier cookie recipes. Alice and Sophia rolled out ropes of red and white cookie dough, twisting them together into the shape of candy canes. Meanwhile, Riley tried to show Jacob all her techniques for rolling perfect sugar cookies. The fragile dough was likely to stick to the rolling pin or tear, making it more complicated than it looked.

"The secret is to just pop the dough in the freezer for a few minutes," Riley explained after the dough tore again. "It has to be nice and cold; otherwise it gets sticky and can tear more easily, and the cookies won't hold their shape when you transfer them to the baking tray."

"Cool," Jacob said.

"It's hard because having the oven on makes the room warmer," Riley continued. "But after a few minutes in the freezer, the dough will be much easier to handle. You'll see."

"How did you learn so much about baking?" asked Jacob.

Riley laughed. "Are you kidding? Christmas cookies are my obsession," she replied.

"Hey, you're not giving yourself enough credit," Sophia spoke up. "*Everything* Christmas is your obsession!"

For the next two hours, the friends baked trays of cookies in shifts—snowballs, then candy canes, then sugar cookies—until all the dough was gone. While the cookies cooled, Riley mixed together several colors of icing: red, pink, yellow, green, white, and blue. Decorating cookies was one of her favorite Christmas activities—and it was even more fun with friends!

When all the cookies had been decorated, the friends packaged them in clear cellophane bags tied up with festive ribbons. Riley plucked her favorite cookie—a snowflake-shaped sugar cookie covered with pale blue icing and silver sprinkles—from the tray and slid it into a special bag.

"Keeping that one for yourself?" Jacob teased her.

"Actually, I'm going to give it to my Secret Snowflake tomorrow," Riley told him. "If that's okay with you?"

"Yeah, sure," Jacob said quickly. "Why wouldn't it be okay?"

"Just checking," Riley said with a shrug. "My Secret Snowflake is going to love it!" she said happily. She was already thinking about how Marcus would react when he found the extra-special, extra-delicious cookie she'd made. She was so excited thinking about Marcus enjoying her cookie that she didn't notice the strange look that had come over Jacob's face.

Chapter 8

It was funny how quickly Riley got in the habit of popping by homeroom at the end of the school day— just to check if there was a surprise waiting in her Secret Snowflake mailbox.

And on Tuesday afternoon, there was!

Riley pulled out a lumpy, soft package wrapped in red-and-green-striped paper. It was heavy in her hands, different from the other gifts she'd received so far—the glitter paper, the light-up Christmas tree pin, the nail polish. She turned the package over in her hands, trying to guess what might be inside. The truth was, though, that Riley didn't have a clue.

She used her blue-painted nail to tear open the back flap of the present and discovered a whole pound of chocolate-chip-cookie-dough-flavored fudge from Creekside Cafe & Chocolates, Hampton Creek's best sweet shop! Riley couldn't believe her Secret Snowflake had given her another perfect present—and the PEANUT FREE label meant she could even share it with her cookie-dough-loving brother.

Riley shoved the fudge into her backpack; she had to hurry because the 3C bus to the Sunny Acres Retirement Community would be leaving soon. She was about to toss the striped wrapping paper into the trash can when she noticed something bright and colorful on the floor nearby. It caught her eye immediately—maybe because she recognized it.

It was a corner of the brightly patterned origami paper she'd used to make Marcus's latest Secret Snowflake gift, an origami skateboarder. The pattern was really tricky, but Riley had persevered— even though it had taken her a few hours and almost an entire package of origami paper to get it right. The best part was that the wheels of the skateboard moved when you pushed it down. She'd thought

Marcus would appreciate it, especially since he loved to skateboard when the weather was nice.

But why was the origami skateboarder forgotten on the floor, next to the trash can like someone had thrown it away—and not even cared enough to make sure it made it in the basket? She had only delivered it a few hours before.

Marcus wouldn't throw away a Secret Snowflake gift, Riley told herself. *He would* never *do that!*

Or would he?

She pushed the thought from her mind as she knelt down to pick up the origami skateboarder. What should she do with it? Keep it? Throw it away? Sneak it into Marcus's desk? Put it back in his Secret Snowflake mailbox?

None of the options seemed quite right. But Riley knew she had to make a decision quickly. The bus would be leaving soon—and she didn't want to be left behind.

It seemed too weird to put the origami skateboarder back in Marcus's Secret Snowflake mailbox, like she was regifting a present he'd already received. And she definitely wasn't going to throw it away.

Riley had spent *way* too many hours on all those precise creases and tricky folds to toss it in the trash. The more she thought about it, the more certain she was that Marcus had simply dropped it. Maybe it had fallen out of his pocket or his backpack. Maybe he and his buddies were goofing around, shoving and pushing each other like they did sometimes, and it had slipped out, and he wouldn't even notice that he'd lost it for hours. Then maybe Marcus would search his backpack like crazy, wondering what could have happened to it.

Don't worry, Marcus, Riley thought with a smile as she slipped the origami skateboarder into his desk. *It will be right here, waiting for you.*

Now Riley really was in danger of missing the bus. She ran all the way to the school parking lot, where the regular buses were already on their way out. Behind the music room, she could see that the 3C bus was idling, puffs of exhaust floating through the frosty air. Riley started running even faster.

"Riley! You made it!" Mr. Mac exclaimed as she clambered up the steps of the bus. "Sophia told us you were coming—"

"I wouldn't miss it for anything," Riley said breathlessly. "Sorry I'm late! Had to—get something—"

"Grab a seat so we can get on the road," Mr. Mac told her.

Riley glanced down the aisle, searching for her friends. She grinned when she saw that Jacob, Sophia, and Alice had snagged the coveted seats at the rear of the bus. Not only were there more windows back there, the ride was bumpier—which made it way more fun.

"Good job on the seats, guys," she said. "Though you've probably made enemies for life with Squad Eight."

Sophia rolled her eyes. "Who cares? Aren't they graduating in a few months?" she asked. "Where were you? We almost had to leave without you!"

Riley didn't want to tell her about Marcus's Secret Snowflake gift, abandoned by the trash can. Instead, she said, "I stopped by my Secret Snowflake mailbox and—well, let's just say you're welcome!"

Riley unzipped her backpack to show everyone the package of fudge.

"You got a whole pound of cookie dough fudge?" Sophia gasped. "Seriously?"

"I know, right?" Riley replied, grinning. "I feel like I hit the Secret Snowflake jackpot!"

"You really did," Sophia said.

"I don't know," Alice spoke up. "Mine is pretty great, too. I found a roll of tokens for the arcade! I didn't even know Hampton Creek had an arcade! What's it called?"

"High Score," Sophia and Riley said at the same time, exchanging a secret smile.

"Wait a second," Jacob spoke up. "You've lived in Hampton Creek since September and you didn't know about the arcade?"

"I guess there were other things higher on my parents' priority list than scoping out the area arcades," Alice said with a laugh. "Finding a grocery store, finding a doctor, finding a vet…"

"High Score is really cool," Sophia said. "We should go sometime, if you want to check it out."

"Thanks—that sounds fun," Alice told her.

"Anyway, I thought we could share some fudge

on the way over to Sunny Acres," Riley said. "We have to save a piece for Theo, though. He's going to freak out when I get home. Peanut-free cookie dough fudge! This will blow his mind!"

After Riley passed out pieces of fudge, the kids were quiet for a moment—the fudge was *that* delicious.

Jacob swallowed his bite and gestured toward the leftover fudge in Riley's backpack. "My mom keeps fudge in the fridge," he said. "It's even better cold."

"Thanks for the pro tip," Riley said.

"Can you believe we have our first 3C performance?" Alice asked Sophia. "We just joined, like, four days ago! I'm kind of nervous!"

"Don't be," Riley assured her. "I mean, it can't possibly be anywhere near as bad as our show at the Hampton Creek Mall."

"Shhh!" Sophia whispered loudly. "Don't jinx us!"

"Riley, you missed us loading the bus," Jacob began. "Everybody brought so much Christmas stuff! You won't believe it."

"Did 3C go Christmas crazy?" Riley asked, giggling.

"Let's just say that our cookies are only the beginning," he replied.

"I saw wreaths, mini-trees, garlands, lights," Sophia said, ticking each one off on her fingers. "Not to mention all the stuff that belonged to Mr. Mac's grandma."

Riley shivered with excitement as the bus pulled up in front of Sunny Acres. She could hardly wait to see how the residents would react to the Christmas surprises 3C had planned for them.

When the bus stopped moving, Mr. Mac stood up with a special announcement.

"Listen up, 3C," he began. "I have one more surprise about this trip."

"What?" all the students called out together.

"We're not just going to sing our songs in the common room like a regular concert—we're going caroling!" Mr. Mac announced.

"Seriously?" Riley exclaimed. She was *not* expecting that their 3C concert would become a caroling party instead!

"That's right—caroling up and down the halls of Sunny Acres," Mr. Mac continued. "The residents have no idea what's in store for them! So here's how it will go: You'll knock on the door, and when they open it, launch into one of the songs—usually a traditional carol is best, but you and your caroling buddy can choose—and make someone's day with your Christmas cheer, okay?"

"Okay!" everyone yelled, so loudly that Mr. Mac pretended to stumble backward.

"I printed out a bunch of invitations to our little soiree in the common room—don't forget to take a stack," he said. "I'm sure the residents will be excited to help us decorate, and maybe they'll even join us in singing some old favorites. This is also a good time to deliver any gifts or surprises you brought, too. Ready? Let's do this!"

The kids filed off the bus. It was clear that pretty much everybody would be caroling with his or her seatmate—which meant that Riley and Jacob would be paired up again. Riley didn't mind. The more time she spent with Jacob, the more she enjoyed hanging out with him.

As the other members of 3C spread out through

the halls, Jacob pointed to the elevator bank. "Want to take this show upstairs?" he asked.

"Sure, why not?" Riley replied. It was a good choice; the second floor was pretty deserted, with long rows of identical gray-green doors on either side of the corridor. A couple of residents had added some forlorn decorations to their doors—a plastic wreath here, a dusty velvet bow there—and Riley made a mental note to ask Mr. Mac if there would be enough decorations to add some to the second floor as well. She was confident that a little extra Christmas cheer was all it would take to transform Sunny Acres into a magical holiday wonderland!

"I've always wanted to go caroling—but now it seems kind of weird," she confided to Jacob as they walked toward the first door. "We just, like, knock on the door and start singing? To strangers?"

"I don't know why you would call that weird," Jacob said wryly. "I'd call it your average Tuesday."

Riley burst out laughing so hard that Jacob, grinning, held a finger to his lips. "Shhh!" he said. "Don't warn them that we're on our way!"

"What are we, ninja carolers?" Riley asked.

"When it comes to Christmas caroling, stealth is almost more important than the singing," Jacob said.

"If you don't stop joking, I won't be able to stop laughing!" Riley replied. "Come on. We have to take it seriously. No more messing around."

"Yes, ma'am," Jacob said, giving Riley a funny salute.

By then, they were standing in front of the first door in the hallway, number 201. A small brass nameplate read MRS. B. RUSSELL.

For a moment, Jacob and Riley just stood there.

"Are you going to knock?" Riley finally asked.

"I thought you were," Jacob replied. "Let's do it together. One, two—"

"Wait!" Riley exclaimed. "We didn't pick a song."

"Oops," Jacob said with a laugh. "What do you want to sing?"

"Hmm," Riley said thoughtfully. "How about 'Here We Come A-Caroling.'"

"I like it," Jacob said, nodding. "Very appropriate. Okay, now, one, two, *three*!"

At the same time, Riley and Jacob rapped on the door.

"Just a minute!" a voice called to them.

This is it, Riley thought, her heart pounding. *Any second, that door will swing wide open, and we'll have an audience of one, and—*

The door opened. A small woman with snow-white hair piled into a bun looked surprised to see Riley and Jacob. "Yes, dears?" she said. "Can I help you?"

Riley took a deep breath, then she and Jacob exchanged a glance. There was the slightest, barely perceptible nod to Jacob's head. Riley could tell it was her cue.

Then they started to sing.

> *Here we come a-caroling*
> *Among the leaves so green,*
> *Here we come a-wandering*
> *So fair to be seen...*

Right before she started to sing, Riley had a brief

flash of worry—*What if this is beyond embarrassing? What if she slams the door in our faces?*—but it faded almost immediately. There was something enchanting, almost magical, about the way Riley's and Jacob's voices rose in a duet, singing each clear, sweet note.

But even better than the sound of their singing was its impact. Mrs. Russell's eyes were wide with delight; her mouth spread into a joyful smile that seemed to capture the very spirit of Christmas. By being part of that—by helping to bring joy to her— Riley's own joy tripled, and she remembered all over again what she loved most about Christmas.

"Oh, wonderful! Simply wonderful!" Mrs. Russell cried, clapping her hands together. "Bravo! Why, I haven't heard carolers in such a long time! Christmas caroling used to be one of my favorite parts of the season. I can't imagine why people don't go caroling like they used to."

"Neither can I," Riley replied. Caroling was even more fun than a regular choral performance. She couldn't wait to knock on the next door. "We have a present for you, too!"

"Christmas cookies! What a treat!" Mrs. Robbins exclaimed. "They look delicious."

Jacob gave Mrs. Robbins one of Mr. Mac's party invitations. "We hope you can join us in the common room for a Christmas party in an hour," he told her.

"I wouldn't miss it," she promised.

"Merry Christmas!" Riley said, waving as Mrs. Robbins closed her door.

Then Riley and Jacob were off to the next apartment, and the next one, and the one after that. Once in a while, they stopped by an empty apartment, but almost everyone opened their doors wide—and delighted in the caroling and the Christmas cookies. The residents were so enthusiastic that Riley wasn't surprised to see that the common room was almost full by the time she and Jacob finished caroling on the second floor. It was hard to tell who enjoyed the party more—the senior citizens or the middle-school students!

Riley was extra glad that she'd finished all her home-work during study hall that afternoon. By the time she got home from the trip to Sunny Acres, the last thing she felt like doing was reading her history textbook or puzzling through her geometry problems. She had a feeling, too, that with Christmas break just three days away, all her teachers had lightened the homework load a little. Who could blame them? Riley was sure they were just as eager for the break as their students—and they probably had more important things to do than grade homework right before Christmas!

Three days, Riley suddenly thought. Three days until Christmas break…three days until the Christmas party at school…three days to deliver one last Secret Snowflake gift…three days until the big reveal.

The book for Marcus was, at best, half finished. Riley had selected all the quotes and poems, and copied them in her best handwriting. But she still had to make the cover, decorate a title page and table of contents, and then assemble the whole thing. It was going to be a *lot* of work…especially without a weekend before the end of Secret Snowflake. Plus, Riley had promised Sophia that she would help her make a special invitation to the New Year's Eve sleepover for Alice. She knew that the silver glitter paper from her first Secret Snowflake gift would be perfect for it.

Despite everything she still had to do, Riley was up for the challenge. She'd put way too much effort and energy into Marcus's Secret Snowflake surprises to do a halfhearted job on the last—and most special—gift of all.

It wasn't until Riley had assembled all her supplies—the rice paper for the interior pages; the acid-free glue; her best calligraphy pen; her sharpest scissors; and, of course, two sheets of glitter paper for the cover—that she realized she hadn't thought about Marcus the entire time she'd been at Sunny Acres.

Not even once.

Chapter 9

Somehow, the teachers expected everyone to be able to focus on schoolwork on Friday, even though it was the last day before break. Even though the best party of the school year—and the long-awaited Secret Snowflake reveal—was right after lunch. Even though the final Secret Snowflake gifts were waiting, wrapped and ready, under Mr. Mac's crazy-looking metal tree in the music room. Riley had seen them when she'd snuck in, just before homeroom, to nestle the book of Christmas poems she'd made for Marcus under the shiny boughs. The handwritten, hand-stitched book was so special to her that she hated to leave it unattended under the tree, even for a few hours. She wished that she could deliver it to Marcus that very minute! But Riley had waited this long. She could manage a few more hours.

The warning bell rang. Riley took one last opportunity to adjust the bow on Marcus's gift before she hurried off to homeroom. Mrs. Darlington was standing at her desk, smiling, with a big box of doughnuts.

"Good morning, class!" she announced as Riley slipped into her seat. But there was so much chatter that no one answered—or even seemed to hear—her.

Mrs. Darlington cleared her throat and tried again, louder this time. "I said, *good morning, class!*"

This time, people started paying attention.

"I know the big party is this afternoon—but I thought we could kick off the celebrations this morning," Mrs. Darlington announced. "Doughnuts for everyone!"

The whole class erupted into cheers!

"But first," Mrs. Darlington continued, "there's one more stage of the Secret Snowflake to complete."

"The reveal?" Ben called out. "Are we gonna find out right now?"

Mrs. Darlington shook her head. "I'm afraid not—that has to wait for the party," she replied. "No, I'd like you to use your class time to write an in-class essay about your experience."

Mrs. Darlington strode over to the podium and switched on the SMART board. She'd already written several prompts.

DID YOU ENJOY SECRET SNOWFLAKE?

WHY OR WHY NOT?

WHAT DID YOU LEARN ABOUT YOUR

SECRET SNOWFLAKE?

WHAT DID YOU LEARN ABOUT YOURSELF?

"Feel free to snack on a doughnut while you write," Mrs. Darlington said. "Just try not to get any crumbs on your essays!"

Riley picked out a doughnut with strawberry glaze and opened her notebook to a fresh piece of paper. She wasn't a big fan of in-class essays—it felt like a lot of pressure, having to write the whole thing in one sitting—but at least for this one, she knew exactly what she wanted to say.

Somehow, each class period ticked away until, at last, even lunch was over—and it was time for the party to begin. Before she went to the music room for the party, Riley popped in the bathroom to make sure she didn't have any food on her face. She stood back and stared at her reflection in the mirror, adjusting her hair—first in front of her shoulders, then behind, then in front again. It was crazy how she looked so, well, *normal* on the outside when she felt like a jangling ball of nervous energy inside.

Because this was it—the moment she'd been imagining for so long. In just minutes, she was going to talk to Marcus. She was going to tell him that she was the one responsible for all his Secret Snowflake gifts. And then she would give him the special book she'd spent so many hours making.

What would happen next? Riley wasn't quite sure. It was the one stage that was difficult—almost impossible—for her to imagine. Marcus would probably confess that he was her Secret Snowflake, too. They would definitely share a laugh about that—after all, what were the odds? Riley didn't know how to calculate them, but she was sure they were tiny. Maybe Marcus would offer to get her something to eat... or maybe he would ask if she wanted to hang out over Christmas break. She really hoped he would. Two weeks without seeing Marcus—without sitting right behind him in first period—felt unbelievably long to Riley. And then... who knew what would happen next?

Riley did know one thing, though.

She wouldn't have to wait much longer to find out.

Riley took a deep breath, squared her shoulders, and nodded at her reflection. *Let's do this*, she thought to herself.

The party was already picking up by the time Riley got to the music room. Mr. Mac, wearing a full Santa suit from head to toe, looked like he was having a blast.

"Merry Christmas, Riley! Ho, ho, ho!" he chortled.

"Merry Christmas, Mr. Mac!" she replied. "When is 3C going to sing?"

Mr. Mac glanced at his watch. "Maybe in ten or fifteen minutes?" he said. "Let's make sure everyone gets here and has a little time to hang out first. Don't go far, though, okay?"

"I won't," Riley promised. She may have missed her cue at the mall, and almost missed the bus to Sunny Acres, but Riley was determined that nothing would interfere with 3C's last performance of the season.

Riley glanced around, admiring how the music room had been transformed. The spindly, silvery tree no longer looked weird; now that it was covered in multicolored Christmas lights, it reflected a beautiful rainbow glow. There was an incredible pile of presents under it, too—all shapes and sizes, wrapped in everything from shiny paper to newspaper comics.

Jazzy versions of Christmas carols were playing from Mr. Mac's laptop. Giant Christmas ornaments they'd made in Ms. Lopez's art class dangled from the ceiling on strands of transparent fishing line, slowly spinning from the invisible air currents circulating around them.

Jacob was near the risers, making sure everyone's music folders were in place. Alice was helping Mrs. Darlington arrange cookies on a platter. Sophia was kneeling by the tree, tidying up the enormous pile of presents. She caught Riley's eye and grinned.

Then Sophia nodded toward the door and gave Riley a subtle thumbs-up. Riley glanced over...

And saw that Marcus had arrived!

Her heartbeat quickened at once. He looked really nice, wearing a dark green shirt with the sleeves rolled up. If Riley just stood there casually, would he notice her? Would he come over to chat?

Maybe, once upon a time, Riley would've waited to find out. But today was different.

Today, she was taking charge.

Riley walked across the room, tossing her hair over her shoulder. "Marcus! Hey!" she said, smiling— but not too big or too toothy. She didn't want to be, like, super obvious or anything.

"What's up, Riley?" Marcus said, smiling back.

He smiled back! she thought, ecstatic.

"Pretty cool party, huh?" Riley asked, plowing

ahead without second-guessing every word that came out of her mouth.

"Yeah, I guess," he replied. "It beats geometry."

Riley laughed. Of course it was better than geometry! Marcus was really funny.

"Countdown to Christmas," Riley said—since they were stating the obvious and all.

"No kidding," Marcus said, shaking his head. "Tomorrow we're leaving for Aspen. I can't wait. Ten days of skiing. I already booked private lessons."

"Wow. That sounds incredible," Riley said, trying to ignore the pang of disappointment. So there'd be no hanging out over Christmas break with Marcus. That was okay. They could still text...if they exchanged numbers before Marcus left.

"You're in that...singing thing, right?" he asked.

Riley's heart leaped. So he *was* paying attention! "Yeah, 3C," she replied. "In fact, we're going to sing at the party. In a little while."

"Cool," Marcus said. He glanced over to the food table.

Think of something to say, Riley ordered herself. *Anything!* It wasn't so easy, though. Riley didn't know if it was because she was nervous, or because she'd had a crush on Marcus for such a long time, but for some reason, carrying on a conversation with him was harder than with anyone else she knew.

"Do you go snowboarding in Aspen, too?" she blurted out. She was pretty sure she already knew the answer, but at least it was something to say. Something to fill the awkward silence between them. Something to keep the conversation going before Marcus broke away and drifted off somewhere else, to talk to someone else....

"You know it!" he said, flashing her that grin that made Riley feel wobbly inside. Then he started going on and on about snowboarding....Riley wanted to pay attention; she *tried* to pay attention, but her mind was already racing ahead. When would she tell Marcus about Secret Snowflake? Was there a casual way to work it into the conversation? She didn't want to wait until after the 3C performance....She didn't want to wait, *period*....

And then Riley realized that she didn't really want to tell him first. She wanted to hear *him* say it.

Go ahead, Riley thought to Marcus. *Tell me. If I'm your Secret Snowflake, say it now.*

"And really, my new snowboard is so much better than all the rest that upgrading was a no-brainer...."

It was useless. Riley could tell she was going to have to help Marcus along.

"Yeah, definitely a no-brainer," she said. "Hopefully you'll have perfect snow in Aspen."

"They make it, you know," Marcus told her. "All the resorts make their own. You can't count on nature, not when it comes to perfect skiing snow."

That was it—her opening.

"So...speaking of snow," Riley said. "Secret Snowflake reveal is coming up, huh? Do you think it will be before or after the performance?"

Marcus shrugged.

"I kind of hope it's before," she heard herself say. "I had the *best* Secret Snowflake. All my presents were amazing. I can't wait to find out who it is!"

Marcus made a face. "You're lucky," he replied. "Mine was the worst!"

Riley blinked. Had she—had she heard him right?

Did he really just say *worst*?

As in, Riley's gifts were the *worst*?

As in, *Riley* was the *worst*?

But—she'd worked so hard—

She had really, really tried—

"Nothing but stupid homemade junk," Marcus was saying. "I don't think my Secret Snowflake spent any money on me!"

Riley felt the color drain from her face; her skin was suddenly cold and clammy.

"I threw one of them away—it was this weird origami thing—and then I found it in my desk the next day," Marcus continued, laughing. "It was like a bad boomerang. I couldn't get rid of it!"

Bad boomerang.

Riley's face didn't feel clammy anymore. Now it was burning like it was on fire. Marcus was still talking, but she wasn't listening; somehow, her brain had managed to shut down her ears, because Riley could not bear to hear one more mocking word—

The book, she thought with a lurching, sick feeling in her stomach.

It was just waiting under the tree, the book in

which she'd invested so much—not just her creativity and her energy and her time, but something more, a small piece of who Riley was inside. In her heart. And one thing was certain—Riley couldn't just leave a piece of her heart under the tree for Marcus to sneer at.

She turned away from him stiffly, not even trusting herself to speak without her voice quavering. Riley's eyes were filling with tears, and she could already tell they were going to feel so good and cool when they spilled onto her burning cheeks—but not here, not in the music room in front of everyone, especially Marcus.

Not here.

Riley walked over to the tree as if she were on autopilot and scooped up the book in one swift motion. She forced herself to walk—slowly and steadily—to the door. But once she was in the hallway, away from all those eyes, she broke into a run.

Chapter 10

Riley didn't know exactly where she was running. If she could've, she would've run all the way home and hidden in her bedroom until, well, forever. Or at least until the new year.

But she couldn't leave school in the middle of the day—not even if she was in danger of dying of embarrassment and the worst hurt feelings she'd ever experienced.

The bathroom was right around the corner. It would have to do.

Riley ducked inside and found, to her relief, that it was deserted; thankfully, everyone else was at the party. She didn't know what she would say or do if someone saw her and asked what was wrong.

Where to begin?

Riley took off her glasses, leaned her head against the cold tile wall, and squeezed her eyes shut. Two tears slipped down her cheeks; Riley sniffed and tried to wipe them away, but more followed.

Stop, she told herself fiercely. What was the point of crying about it? It was too late now; Secret Snowflake was already ruined; all the gifts she'd made for Marcus were basically hated. Tears weren't going to make things better. Riley would need to travel back in time and get a giant do-over, because she should've done everything—every single thing— differently.

But that was a silly dream. A stupid wish. She couldn't undo, couldn't fix anything. She definitely couldn't forget the way Marcus had talked about all the gifts she'd made. Like they were worthless. Like they were less than worthless.

But not this one, Riley thought, staring at the book in her hands. She was glad that she'd rescued it from the tree—and saved it from more of Marcus's mockery.

She flipped through it randomly, scanning the pages, searching for—what? Riley wasn't quite sure. One of the verses, from a poem called "On Giving," caught her attention. Riley paused to read it.

Let all your troubles
melt away,

Like snowflakes
on a sunny day.

A gift from the heart,
beyond all measure,

Is worth far more
than any treasure.

Suddenly, Riley's eyes felt a lot less watery. She read the words again and didn't feel like crying anymore.

The things I made weren't worthless, Riley thought. *They were priceless.*

Why was she standing alone in the bathroom, crying, blaming herself for ruining Secret Snowflake? She'd done her part. She'd been the best friend she could possibly be—and not just to Marcus, but to Sophia and Jacob and even Alice, who she barely knew before Secret Snowflake began.

Riley raised her head, put her glasses back on, and looked at her tear-streaked face in the bathroom mirror. *I'm not embarrassed*, she thought. *He should be embarrassed!*

Marcus might have forgotten that Secret Snowflake wasn't about getting gifts—but Riley sure hadn't. Maybe if he'd been less worried about how much each one had cost, he might have noticed how much time and energy she put into them. He might even have noticed how each one was specially made for him and him alone. Marcus talked a lot about how much things cost, Riley suddenly realized, as if that mattered. And he focused an awful lot on things that Riley didn't really care about—and that was fine, but it made her start to doubt how much she had assumed they had in common. Sure, she could be interested in someone who loved sports—but not someone who measured worth in dollars and cents. And definitely not someone who would throw a handmade gift in the trash like it was garbage.

Secret Snowflake˙ had been really special to Riley—every moment of it—and she wasn't going to let Marcus's rudeness take that away from her. All those moments, daydreaming and planning and imagining...all those hours spent crafting, one of Riley's favorite things to do...

Not to mention all the thrilling wonder about her Secret Snowflake's real identity, which had added so much extra sparkle to the season.

Riley paused. *Marcus* wasn't *my Secret Snowflake*, she realized. If it had been Marcus, of course, he would have told her right then and there—not started trashing the gifts *he'd* received.

Besides, Riley's Secret Snowflake was someone who was kind and thoughtful. Which—she now knew—ruled Marcus out entirely.

Riley grabbed a paper towel and ran it under cool water. She wiped her face and looked at herself in the mirror again. *No more tears*, she thought. Her face already looked less red. She took a few deep breaths. Was she ready to go back to the party? She wanted to know, more than anything, who'd left her those special gifts. If she went back to the party, she'd be able to find out. Whoever it was, they were a lot more deserving of Riley's time than Marcus. Maybe if Riley had been paying more attention to who Marcus really was—instead of who she wanted him to be—she would have realized all that sooner. *Better late than never*, she thought.

"The concert!" Riley suddenly gasped out loud, her words echoing off the tile walls. She'd rushed out of the music room so fast that she had forgotten all about the 3C performance—the very last one of the year. She couldn't bear to miss it—not over someone like Marcus.

But Mr. Mac had said that 3C would sing on the early side—maybe just ten minutes into the party. Was Riley too late? Was the performance already under way? Or—worse—over already?

She wanted to sing, now more than ever.

She at least had to try to make it in time!

After one last glance in the mirror to make sure it didn't look she'd been crying, Riley flew out of the girls' bathroom and raced through the hall so fast that she nearly skidded in her sparkly shoes. She strained her ears listening, desperately hoping that she wouldn't hear the strains of 3C singing one of their songs. So far, so good...

Riley was breathless by the time she reached the music room. She didn't hear anything—but through the narrow window in the door, she could see that everyone in 3C had assembled on the risers. Mr. Mac was at the keyboard, getting ready to play....

Riley scurried in and pushed through the crowd. "Sorry—oops—excuse me, sorry!" she murmured as she made her way to the risers. Sophia gave her a look—half exasperation, half relief—as she moved aside to make room for Riley to reach her spot. Then Sophia gave her a half shrug with her palms up, as if to say, "What happened?"

"Tell you later," Riley mouthed as she took her place next to Jacob.

Riley exhaled, hard, and glanced over at Mr. Mac. She wanted to tell him she was sorry for being late—for almost missing the performance—but when he smiled warmly at her, she realized she didn't need to apologize. That was the real Christmas spirit, of course, and the shock of Marcus's meanness had almost made her forget. Christmas, first and foremost, was about kindness and compassion. Forgiveness and understanding.

It was about love, in all its wondrous forms.

"Glad you made it," Jacob whispered in the moment before Mr. Mac started to play.

"Me too," Riley whispered back.

The first chords filled the air. Riley opened her music folder, and—at the exact moment, in just the right way—she sang. The magic that happened when

3C sang had never been more powerful. Riley could hear, faintly, her own voice, but what was really amazing was the way it was one small part of a much greater whole. This was no time for a solo, not when *all* the voices could come together and sound *that* incredible.

The kids—the ones who were watching—could feel it, too. Some people in 3C had worried that they'd be laughed at when they sang at the party. It was one thing to sing at a nursing home, or even at the mall, but in middle school? Forget it.

It was clear now that those worries were unfounded. Riley looked out into the audience and saw that the other students were rocking out along with 3C. Somewhere out there, she knew, was her Secret Snowflake. Soon she'd know who it was. When the performance was over, and the last gifts had been exchanged...

Next to her, Jacob shifted his weight from one foot to the other. For the briefest moment, Riley felt his arm brush against hers. Lightning struck then, an electric shock that started in Riley's brain and zipped all the way down to her fingertips. As the feeling subsided, Riley was left with a single thought in her mind.

Was *Jacob* her Secret Snowflake?

Had he been right there by her side all along?

Chapter 11

It took all of Riley's concentration to get through the rest of the songs and not let her mind wander with thoughts about Jacob. Right now, 3C demanded—and deserved—her full attention. There would be time afterward, Riley knew, to find out the truth.

Then they were singing the last note of the last song, which seemed to hang in the air, quivering, until it faded away. There was half a second of silence, then everyone in the room burst into the wildest, most thunderous applause Riley had ever heard. Riley grinned at the audience, not caring if her smile was too big. It could never be big enough to capture everything Riley was feeling in that moment: her gratitude for the gift of song, her pride in a successful performance, and, most of all, her joy.

"Thank you, thank you, thank you!" Mr. Mac announced to the crowd. "Before we get back to the party, I'm going to turn it over to Mrs. Darlington."

"Let's have another round of applause for 3C!" she said. "That performance was incredible!"

Everybody started clapping and cheering again.

"And now, the moment you've all been waiting for," Mrs. Darlington continued. "At last, you'll find out the identity of your Secret Snowflakes. I'm looking forward to reading your in-class essays over the break. I hope that participating in Secret Snowflake has been as fun and meaningful for you as it has been for me."

Huh? Riley thought. *Mrs. Darlington didn't have a Secret Snowflake partner. How was it fun for her?*

"I've loved every minute, from seeing you sneak into class early to deliver your gifts in secret to overhearing your whispered plans for kindness and generosity. My hope for the coming year is that these new friendships born from Secret Snowflake will only grow stronger," Mrs. Darlington said. "Now, go ahead—find your Secret Snowflake and tell them everything!"

There was a tremendous flurry of activity in the music room as the other kids scrambled around, looking for their Secret Snowflake and exchanging the final presents. Riley stood very still, keenly aware of Jacob beside her. If he was her Secret Snowflake—if he'd been giving her all those incredible gifts—now would be the perfect time to tell her.

But Jacob clambered down the risers like everyone else.

Riley was surprised by the sudden swell of disappointment she felt. *It's just . . . everything*, she told herself. All the late nights working on the Secret Snowflake presents, the weeks of anticipation, the incredible performance. No wonder her emotions were on a total roller coaster.

Riley climbed down the risers, one careful step at a time, and waited off to the side. She felt kind of funny, just standing around when there was so much bustling activity around her. She tucked the special book she'd made under her arm and tried to figure out what to do next. She wasn't about to go find Marcus—she was *done* with him—which meant she had to wait for her Secret Snowflake to find her.

Riley glanced around the room. She spotted Sophia giving Alice the invitation to their New Year's Eve sleepover party and smiled as Alice squealed and gave Sophia a big hug. Riley was delighted to see Alice so excited. She could already tell the three of them were going to have an incredible time at the sleepover party!

Is my Secret Snowflake absent today? Riley wondered. She felt so dumb, just standing there. Maybe it would be less conspicuous if she leaned against the wall...or found a place to sit....

Riley took a step back to sit on the bottom level of the risers—and stumbled right into someone. "Oh! Sorry!" she cried.

Someone's hand reached out to grab her elbow,

steadying her. She looked up...right into Jacob's hazel eyes.

"Sorry," Riley apologized again. "I didn't mean to get in your way."

"You're not in my way," he said in a quiet voice.

There was a pause. Riley wondered...but she had been wrong about Marcus already. She didn't want to be wrong again—especially not this time.

Jacob opened his mouth to say something, but closed it quickly and kind of rolled his eyes. "I'm... not good at this," he said, almost laughing at himself. "Here. This is for you."

He held out a small envelope.

Riley took it, a little unsure. Was this the big reveal? Was Jacob really her Secret Snowflake?

She lifted the flap and pulled out a gift card to the Cupcakery and suddenly, in a flash, remembered talking about the Cupcakery during one of their 3C rehearsals....

And the quest for peanut-free treats the whole family could enjoy...right before the peanut-free fudge showed up in her Secret Snowflake mailbox....

And the way Jacob had been weirdly curious

about her festive wear...right before she'd received the light-up Christmas tree pin....

And the sparkly nail polish...and the sparkly paper, two sheets of which made up the cover for the book that was tucked under Riley's arm at that very moment....

"It was you?" she exclaimed.

Jacob nodded, smiling and blushing at the same time. "It was me," he said. He gestured to the gift card. "I almost got you a dozen cupcakes but then I thought, you know, maybe you'd rather eat there instead. With Marcus. I can tell you sort of...like him."

Of course that's what you thought, Riley realized. Because Jacob was kind, because he was caring, because he was always thinking about others before himself.

"Actually," Riley said, "I think I'd rather go with you."

He was so surprised—and Riley loved how surprised he was; it was so cute—that for a moment he just stood there as a slow smile crossed his face.

"Will you be around over Christmas break?" Riley asked.

"Y-yeah," Jacob replied. "Definitely. We can definitely get cupcakes."

"Text me over break and we'll get together for sure," Riley said. She was now painfully aware of the book under her arm. She could...but what if he... then again...

Don't obsess, Riley told herself. She remembered the inscription she'd written: *For someone who captures the spirit of Christmas in everything he does.* Those words described Jacob better than anyone else she knew. Maybe, somehow, the book she'd made was meant for Jacob all along. After all, hadn't he slipped a poem into each and every one of her Secret Snowflake presents?

"I have something for you, too," Riley said. Shyly, she held out the book. "Merry Christmas."

"Wow," Jacob said. "This is incredible. Did you— you *made* it?"

Riley nodded.

"I can't accept it," Jacob continued. "It's too nice."

Kind of like you, Riley thought. But what she said was, "I want you to have it. Look at it this way—if you accept it, it's like you're giving me one last Secret Snowflake present."

Jacob raised an eyebrow. "Last?" he said. "Who said anything about last?"

Riley smiled. She had a feeling Jacob was right.

After all, they were just getting started!

Not finished celebrating the season yet? Here's a sneak peek at another book in the series:

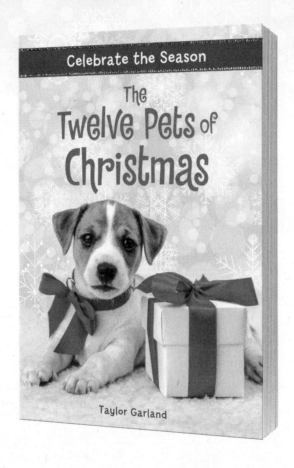

Celebrate the Season

The
Twelve Pets of
Christmas

Taylor Garland

The Twelve Pets of Christmas

Quinn Cooper didn't even want to blink. If she blinked, she might miss something—and there was so much to see! Finer Arts, the art supply store in Quinn's hometown of Marion, was her favorite place in the whole world.

Quinn trailed through each aisle—past the vibrant rainbow of paints; past the colored pencils in every hue imaginable; past handmade paper flecked with bits of gold and silver; past the long strands of glittering crystal beads. Every aisle inspired Quinn to start a new project. But now, she knew, was not the time. Not when she had so much to do!

Reluctantly, Quinn tore herself away from the

handspun yarn section and headed toward the counter. The store's owner, Ms. Morimoto, smiled as Quinn approached.

"Hi, Quinn! I have a surprise for you," Ms. Morimoto began.

Quinn's eyes lit up. "Did they come? Did they come?" she exclaimed.

"Voilà!" Ms. Morimoto announced as she pulled a red box from under the counter. Her eyes were twinkling as she passed it to Quinn. "Careful, now... they're very fragile."

Quinn held her breath as she eased off the lid. Nestled inside the box were twelve perfectly round ornaments, each one made of delicate blown glass. The ornaments reflected the bright lights overhead, but otherwise they were completely blank.

"They're perfect!" Quinn exclaimed. "Thank you, Ms. Morimoto!"

"It's my pleasure," the older woman replied. "I always try to make sure our special orders arrive as quickly as possible."

"The timing is *perfect*," Quinn said. "I'll be able to paint them over Thanksgiving break!"

"Are they for your family's Christmas tree?" asked Ms. Morimoto.

Quinn shook her head. "I'm going to donate them to the Marion Animal Shelter's fund-raiser," she replied. "They're kicking off a special event this year—the Twelve Pets of Christmas."

"Oh, yes—I've seen the flyers," Ms. Morimoto replied. "Tell me more."

"Mrs. Alvarez—she's the shelter director—well, she had this amazing idea," Quinn began. "The Twelve Pets of Christmas is a big promotional campaign to encourage people to adopt pets instead of buying them from a store. It kicks off with a fancy fund-raiser in ten days! There's going to be food, and dancing, and special Christmas cookies, and an auction with some really cool stuff, and portraits of the Twelve Pets that we especially hope will be adopted before Christmas. I'm donating twelve hand-painted ornaments. I'm going to paint animals on them."

"Genius!" Ms. Morimoto said. "I'm so impressed that you're using your artistic talents for such a good cause, Quinn."

"It's the least I can do," Quinn said. "I love helping

out at the animal shelter after school. And that's not all! At the benefit, I'll be—"

Quinn's voice trailed off abruptly.

"On second thought, maybe you could come see for yourself?" she continued. Quinn rummaged around in her backpack until she found a ticket to the fund-raiser. "All the volunteers got two free tickets. Would you like one of mine?"

Ms. Morimoto looked surprised, but only for a moment. Then a broad smile crossed her face. "I'd love to come. Thanks, Quinn!" she said as she took the ticket.

"Great! And that way, you can see all the finished ornaments, too," Quinn replied. "I hope they turn out okay. I've never painted on glass before."

"I'm sure they'll be beautiful!" Ms. Morimoto assured her. "Just remember that the colors you use will shift a little, depending on the color of the ornament. And, you know, you could always add a little..."

Quinn waited expectantly while Ms. Morimoto reached under the counter again.

"Here you go—on the house." Ms. Morimoto

gave Quinn a small jar of crystal glitter. "It's Christmas," she finished. "There's no such thing as too much sparkle!"

"Thank you!" Quinn said.

"Just sprinkle it on while the paint's still wet and you'll be good to go," Ms. Morimoto told her. "I'll see you at the benefit—and all your ornaments, too!"

"Bye, Ms. Morimoto," Quinn said as she carefully cradled the box of ornaments in her arms. "Thanks again—for everything!"

"Stay warm," Ms. Morimoto called out. "It looks like it's going to snow."

"I hope so!" Quinn said, laughing. "Bye!"

When Quinn stepped outside, she realized that it didn't just *look* like snow; it smelled like snow, too. That crisp, cold tang in the air was instantly recognizable. In her warm parka, Quinn didn't mind the chilly temperatures as she walked a couple of blocks home to the condo where she lived with her dad and their pet cat, Piper. It would be unusual to get a big snowstorm before Thanksgiving—but not impossible. Quinn couldn't help grinning as she remembered the massive blizzard that had hit Marion last winter, closing school for an entire week! Quinn and her best friend, Annabelle, had gone sledding on the big hill in Center Park for hours. Then, because school was closed, Annabelle got to sleep over at Quinn's house for two nights in a row!

It was a great memory—but it made Quinn a little sad, too. If there was a big snowstorm this year, she and Annabelle wouldn't be sledding together, and Annabelle wouldn't be spending the night. Just three months ago, Annabelle had moved all the way to California...and Quinn had no idea when they would get to see each other again. That was one of the reasons why Quinn was so grateful for the opportunity to volunteer at the animal shelter. Playing with the kittens always made her laugh, and she loved taking the dogs for walks in the neighborhood. Quinn knew how important it was to shower the shelter animals with lots of love and care while they waited to be adopted. Happy animals were much more likely to be adopted—and happy animals knew that they were loved. Most of all, though, staying busy helped Quinn keep her mind off how much she missed Annabelle.

"Hey, Dad!" Quinn called out as she walked through the front door.

"Hey, Q!" he called back from his office. As an illustrator, Quinn's dad worked from home in an office that was nearly as well stocked as Ms. Morimoto's store.

"Look—my ornaments came!" Quinn announced as she carefully placed the box on the kitchen table.

"Great news," Dad said as he appeared in the doorway. "I had a feeling Ms. Morimoto would come through for you."

"Four days with no school, no homework, nothing but painting…" Quinn said in a dreamy voice. "One more day until Thanksgiving break, and I can't wait!"

She snuck a glance at the clock. Technically, the rule was that Quinn had to finish her homework before she could paint or draw, but maybe Dad would make an exception today.

As if Dad could read her mind, he laughed. "Go ahead, Q," he said. "I don't see why you can't do your homework after dinner today."

"How did you know what I was thinking?" Quinn asked, smiling.

"You got that look in your eyes," he said knowingly. "That *I can't wait to get started* gleam. I recognized it right away."

Quinn crossed the room to give her dad a big hug. "Thanks, Dad," she said. "I promise I'll get all my homework done after dinner. And I'll do the dishes, too!"

"Even better!" Dad joked.

Quinn scooped up the ornaments and hurried back to her room. It was hard for Quinn to keep her desk tidy—it was always cluttered with school papers, pencils, and books—but she kept her art table perfectly organized. When she had the urge to paint or draw, the last thing Quinn wanted to do was waste time cleaning up!

Quinn's acrylic paints were already arranged in rainbow order. She'd picked out a few metallic accent colors, too—silver, gold, and crimson—which shimmered under the bright light as she poured little pools of paint onto her palette. Then Quinn picked out a gold ornament from the box. She stared at it, deep in thought, as she tried to decide what, exactly, she would paint there.

Tap. Tap. Tap.

Quinn didn't even notice that she was tapping the end of her paintbrush against the side of her palette. *The gold ornament reminds me of Annabelle's dog, Bumblebee,* she thought. *But if I paint him, he'll blend right into the ornament.*

But there was no reason Quinn couldn't paint a dark brown dog instead!

Quinn had been painting animals for ages—especially her friends' pets—so it wasn't too hard for her to paint a chocolate-brown version of Bumblebee. She grinned to herself as she made one of the dog's ears flop the wrong way. It made the dog on the ornament look curious and playful—and ready for fun!

I have got to text a picture of this to Annabelle, Quinn thought as she examined her work. But the ornament didn't feel quite finished. There was something missing... but what?

It's not festive enough, Quinn suddenly realized. With quick, sure strokes, she painted a wreath of dark green leaves around the dog's face. Then she added a few bright red holly berries for a pop of color.

"Less is more" was one of those things adults

liked to say, and most of the time, Quinn couldn't disagree more. Fewer chocolate chips in a cookie and less frosting on a cupcake were definitely *not* better than the opposite.

But when it came to artwork, Quinn knew it was usually true. Sure, she could add more and more decoration to the gold ornament, but something deep inside told her that it was just right—just the way it was.

And just in time, too, as Dad called to Quinn from the kitchen, "Dinner's ready!"

Quinn carefully nestled the ornament back in the box, with the painted side up so that it wouldn't smudge. One down...eleven to go. Quinn couldn't wait to find out what she'd paint next!